## The Princess Sister Swap

Clem Beaumont and Princess Arrosa Artega, half sisters united by a strong and loving bond but kept apart by circumstances beyond their control. With pressure growing on Arrosa to marry, Clem hatches an audacious plan to temporarily swap their lives, giving Arrosa one final summer of freedom in Cornwall and allowing Clem to spend time in the beautiful country of Asturia, a place denied to her all of her life!

But their simple—if risky—plan begins to unravel when Arrosa and Clem unexpectedly meet the men of their dreams...

Read Clem and Akil's story in
*Cinderella and the Vicomte*

And Arrosa and Jack's story in
*The Princess and the Single Dad*

Both available now from Harlequin Romance!

Dear Reader,

Welcome to part two of The Princess Sister Swap.

One of my favorite films is *Roman Holiday*, not just because Gregory Peck is gorgeous and Audrey Hepburn utterly beautiful, but because it's so bittersweet. Much as Audrey Hepburn's princess adores every moment of her escape into Rome, she knows that duty calls in the end. And that's how it is for Arrosa, the heroine of the second book in this series. She is loving her time in Cornwall masquerading as Clem's cousin Rosy, and she's enjoying getting to spend time with handsome tycoon Jack Treloar and his two adorable daughters, but she knows that eventually she has to go back to Asturia and take up her role as the Crown Princess.

I loved revisiting Clem, Arrosa and Asturia, exploring what happened when Arrosa was in Cornwall, and peeking into Clem and Akil's future, and it's always a joy to spend time in Cornwall, even if it is in my imagination. I hope you enjoy Arrosa and Jack's story as much as I enjoyed writing it.

Love,

*Jessica*

# The Princess and the Single Dad

Jessica Gilmore

HARLEQUIN

*Romance*

**HARLEQUIN**®

*Romance*™

Recycling programs
for this product may
not exist in your area.

ISBN-13: 978-1-335-73673-4

The Princess and the Single Dad

Copyright © 2022 by Jessica Gilmore

For questions and comments about the quality of this book, please contact us at CustomerService@Harlequin.com.

Harlequin Enterprises ULC
22 Adelaide St. West, 41st Floor
Toronto, Ontario M5H 4E3, Canada
www.Harlequin.com

Printed in U.S.A.

Incorrigible lover of a happy-ever-after, **Jessica Gilmore** is lucky enough to work for one of London's best-known theaters. Married with one daughter, one fluffy dog and two dog-loathing cats, she can usually be found with her nose in a book. Jessica writes emotional romance with a hint of humor, a splash of sunshine, delicious food—and equally delicious heroes!

### Books by Jessica Gilmore

### Harlequin Romance

#### *The Princess Sister Swap*

*Cinderella and the Vicomte*

#### *Billion-Dollar Matches*

*Indonesian Date with the Single Dad*

#### *Fairytale Brides*

*Cinderella's Secret Royal Fling*
*Reawakened by His Christmas Kiss*
*Bound by the Prince's Baby*

*Summer Romance with the Italian Tycoon*
*Mediterranean Fling to Wedding Ring*
*Winning Back His Runaway Bride*
*Christmas with His Cinderella*

Visit the Author Profile page
at Harlequin.com for more titles.

This book is for everyone who has been able to escape from the trials of the last couple of years through reading romance. Here's to escapism and brighter days.

# CHAPTER ONE

JACK TRELOAR SAT back in the rather uncomfortable stone seat and surveyed his fellow audience members. No surprises here. The audience was exactly what he had expected, people from the village and the surrounding towns, mostly friends and family of the cast, together with a smattering of tourists. An easily pleased, uncritical, warm audience predisposed to be supportive of the amateur production.

Everything he wanted to change.

Although he had to admit to being pleasantly surprised by the performance itself. Yes, it was amateurish, yes, the costumes were clearly home-made, and the backdrops and props owed more to enthusiasm than skill, but some of the acting was really good, good enough to transport him—momentarily—from noticing the chill of the stone seat and the laboured scene changes. Juliet was especially good, although that was no real surprise. After all, Clem Beaumont was a professional, one who, in Jack's opinion, should go back to finding proper paid work and spend less time poking her nose into his business.

At least what he *hoped* would be his business if he could just win round the very community sitting here to his vision. He allowed his gaze to wander around the auditorium once again. This place was a gem, an open-air amphitheatre, stone seats rising up from a semi-circular stage, the sea visible beyond creating a truly atmospheric backdrop as the early June sky began to tinge pink, the sun sinking at last.

At least, it should be a gem. But right now it was more unpolished diamond than jewel in the village crown. Ticket-buyers for the pitifully few shows put on here headed in through a plain reception area where, instead of a bar and restaurant, volunteers sold lukewarm white wine and cans of beer from a trestle table. There was nowhere to mingle, to enjoy an interval drink, to soak up the atmosphere. But the potential was here for anyone with half an eye—and Jack had that eye. He could turn this theatre and Polhallow into a *destination*. A place people flocked to not just for the sea, beautiful as it was, or for the scenery or any of the other reasons that made the Cornish village such an attractive place to holiday, but for the theatre, just as people visited St Ives for art or Padstow for food. Jack had done his research; the stage was big enough to tempt the major touring companies, and the venue could host bands as well as musicals and plays. He could put Polhallow on the map.

But to say that the local community didn't share his vision would be putting it mildly; you'd think he was planning on tearing the whole thing down and replacing it with some kind of concrete monstrosity rather than trying to bring jobs and prosperity to the village outside the crucial summer season. He'd even guaranteed that the local schools, dance troupes and amateur companies could still use the theatre—so why couldn't the village see that everyone would benefit? Probably because he was the one behind the scheme. Clearly it didn't matter how rich and successful he was, the people of Polhallow would only ever see him as the town tearaway.

Well, they would learn to look again. Polhallow was the right place to raise his daughters—

fresh air, outdoor pursuits and less of the monied hedonism that characterised their affluent London neighbourhood. If he had to win the townsfolk round to smooth his daughters' path then that was what he would do. Not that he would mind seeing respect, no matter how grudging, in the eyes of everyone who had doubted or judged him in the past.

Jack had intended to leave at the interval but, despite himself, he found himself getting caught up in the tragedy unfolding on the stage, even though he knew all too well where teen melodrama could lead. The play was brought to life by Clem's charisma and skill and the rest of the cast rose to meet her, some of them achieving what Jack suspected were hitherto unexpected heights. By the time Juliet collapsed on her lover's tomb and the final epilogue was spoken, Jack was shocked to feel the prickling of tears in his eyes. He looked around hurriedly, hoping nobody had seen the weakness. He needn't have worried, because although his presence had attracted a few stares and pointed comments when he'd arrived, most people were too absorbed in the play to give him more than a second glance and were now applauding the cast with gusto.

The woman sitting next to Jack was no exception. She was on her feet clapping and whooping as if she had been watching the Royal Shakespeare Company, tears trickling down her cheeks, visible despite her huge sunglasses, her shouts of 'Bravo! Bravo!' ringing out. She sat back down, removing her sunglasses to quickly wipe away the tears, and caught Jack's amused gaze with a slightly self-deprecating shrug.

'Wasn't that amazing?' She spoke English fluently and with no real discernible accent but there was a trace of something he couldn't place, almost Spanish, or southern French.

'It wasn't what I expected,' Jack said diplomatically. Amazing was maybe pushing it, but he couldn't deny the play hadn't been the car crash he had been expecting.

'Clem is so talented, I had no idea.' The woman continued clapping again enthusiastically and bouncing to her feet as the lead actress came forward. There was a definite similarity between the smiling actress and his neighbour, both had long dark curls and a similar slant to their high cheek-boned oval faces with long-lashed hazel eyes above full mouths. A sense of recognition tugged at him.

'Have we met?' Jack asked.

She shook her head, replacing the sunglasses firmly. 'I don't think so, I'm not from around here. I'm a cousin of Clem's.'

'That explains the resemblance,' he said, and she smiled but with a hint of nervousness that surely his innocuous comment couldn't have provoked.

'Are you staying here long?'

'No.' She slumped very slightly, her tone dejected. 'I have to get back; you know how it is. Duty calls, but I wish I could stay. There is something so special about Polhallow, don't you think? I would love to spend more time here.'

'I know what you mean. I just moved back from London, and I can't believe it's taken me so long.' It was definitely the right idea to move his family back to Cornwall. London felt too big, too dirty, too dangerous for his girls. He wanted them to grow up with beaches to play on and with sea air filling their lungs.

Of course, their childhood was very different to his, thanks to the big clifftop house, the swimming pool and treehouse, the playroom filled with everything their hearts desired. Jack knew the dangers of spoiling his girls, but he also knew what it was like to go without, and it was hard not to be indulgent when they'd lost their mother at such a tender age. He wanted to give them everything he had never had—including a name that was respected. His fortune and success impressed some people, but to far too many he was still that wild Treloar boy.

The cast had taken their final bow and moved off the stage and the audience around them began to move. 'It was nice meeting you.' He held out a hand. 'I'm Jack Treloar. Have a good rest of your visit and do pass my congratulations on to Clem. She's quite something.'

The woman hesitated before taking his hand. As his hand closed round her soft, cool fingers a tingle shot up his arm, unexpected and potent, and it was all he could do not to drop her hand; it had been a long time since he'd had such a powerful physical reaction to a woman, not since Lily. Sometimes he thought that part of him had been buried with his wife.

'Rosy,' she said after a brief pause. 'My friends call me Rosy.' A flower name. His chest squeezed. His wife had insisted on flower names for their daughters, to mirror hers.

'Nice to meet you, Rosy. If you find yourself making a longer stay than expected, look me up. I'd love to buy you a drink.'

Rosy looked as astonished by his offer as he felt having made it. He had been a married man since he was just eighteen thanks to an unplanned pregnancy, widowed for just two years. Jack couldn't remember the last time he'd asked a woman out. Dimples flashed in her cheeks, adding an elfin charm to her undeniable beauty.

'That's a very kind offer, Jack. Maybe one day I'll be able to take you up on it.' She nodded towards the exit. 'I need to go. Enjoy the rest of your evening.'

Jack watched the slim, graceful woman make her way out and a wry smile twisted his mouth. The first time in years he'd been tempted to make a move on a woman, and she couldn't get out of there fast enough.

*Nice job, Treloar.*

He watched her for another couple of seconds before making his own way out of the theatre, acknowledging the few who acknowledged him but not stopping to join any of the chattering groups. He wouldn't be welcome anyway. Besides, he was keen to get home and check in on his sleeping girls, to drop a kiss on their foreheads and whisper his daily affirmation that he was here, and they were safe.

Glancing towards the exit Rosy had disappeared through, he headed in the opposite direction towards home. He was unlikely to see her again and that was a good thing. He didn't have time to date. His family came first, his business second and restoring his name third. That was his choice and he stood by it.

But part of him was still disappointed that they wouldn't have time for that drink before Clem's mysterious cousin disappeared again.

Arrosa Artega, soon to be the Crown Princess of Asturia, made it back to the little clifftop cottage where Clem lived before her half-sister and let herself in with the key she valued far more than any of her heirloom jewels. Henri, her ever-present driver and bodyguard, manoeuvred the bulky hamper she'd brought with her into the house before returning to guard the outside while Arrosa poured herself a glass of wine and curled up on the sofa in the sitting room waiting for Clem to return.

Maybe it was foolishness to risk exposing Clem's identity for such a fleeting visit, but Arrosa hadn't seen her sister in so long. She'd wanted to see her sister act, true, but she was also in a real tangle and Clem was the person who always helped her see straight.

As she sipped the wine she looked around the cosy room with its filled bookshelves and colourful paintings, Gus, the latest in a string of rescue cats, asleep on the window seat. This cottage always felt like home to her, far more than the luxurious château in which she had been raised, and she would always be grateful to Clem's mother for letting her be part of the family, even if Arrosa's—and Clem's—father, Zorien, had deceived the French woman about who he was, and then paid her off to keep Clem's existence a secret. The room was filled with Simone Beaumont's eclectic taste, reflecting her larger-than-life personality, and Arrosa's heart ached with grief for the woman who had been a second mother to her, remembering the summers she had spent here and Simone's warm wisdom and affection.

She was still lost in memory when she heard the sounds of Clem's return and jumped up to embrace her before standing back to examine her closely, drinking in the sister she barely saw.

'It's not that I'm not happy to see you, Rosy,

but what on earth are you doing here?' Clem asked as Arrosa handed her a glass of wine.

'Apart from watching my sister play Juliet? Clem, you were brilliant.'

'You've never come to see me act before.'

Guilt hit her hard as she curled back up on the sofa. 'I wish I had. Clem, I'm so sorry I didn't come to Simone's funeral. I loved her so much, but…'

'That's okay, she would have understood. And you sent such beautiful flowers.'

'But you're my sister, I should have been there for you.'

'It's hard for you to get away. I know that.'

It was, but that was no real excuse, not when Clem needed her. 'It was easier when we were children,' she said wistfully. 'Especially when I was at school and could spend my exeat weekends here as well as some of the holidays.' It had been eight long years since she had last spent time here in Polhallow as plain Rosy, Clem's French cousin. In her memory every day had been sunny and filled with laughter and happiness. The joy of being just Rosy, not a princess.

Clem came and sat next to her, squeezing her hand. 'Fess up, why are you here, apart from coming to see me as Juliet? Don't think

I'm not pleased to see you, but I know you and impulsive isn't in your schedule. Is everything okay?'

Arrosa took a swig of wine and summoned up the courage to say the words she had barely dared to think, memories of her conversation with Akil Ortiz echoing through her mind. 'I'm not sure.' She paused and glanced at her sister. 'I think I just asked someone to marry me.'

'You *think* or you did? Are congratulations in order? Who is the lucky man?' She could hear the worry in Clem's voice and tried not to wince.

'Akil. He's the Vicomte d'Ortiz, a rising star of the opposition. His father, the Duc d'Ortiz, was one of Papa's most vocal critics. Our families have been enemies for generations, you know how Asturians can be, but Akil and I are friends of a sort. We have a lot in common. Family honour and expectations and that kind of thing.'

'Friends of a sort? You're not even dating? Besides, what do you mean, you *think* you asked him to marry you?'

Feeling suddenly overwhelmingly weary, Arrosa tried to find the words to explain how helpful Akil had been in unifying the opposition parties behind the new inheritance law that was due to be ratified at the end of the summer. A law that would change the course of her already restricted life, undoing the primogeniture laws and making her the official heir to the throne.

'Clem, everyone—my parents, my advisers, the newspapers—have been pushing me to marry,' she went on, taking another sip of her wine as her stomach knotted with apprehension about the weeks and months and years ahead. 'To start thinking about an heir of my own. And the country will see me as more settled, more mature if I am married. I don't like being rushed, but I see the sense in it. The problem is, not only am I single but I don't see that changing. On the rare occasion I meet someone I like, the whole princess thing scares them off. Queen-to-be is going to make that a hundred times worse.' She sighed. 'I like Akil and he understands the court and my world and we have similar ambitions for Asturia... We were talking about what I wanted to achieve as the heir and realised how aligned our goals were, and I suddenly thought, well, he's the right age, single, understands my world. I could do a lot worse.' But even as she said the words, she could hear how hollow they were, how defeatist. She wasn't quite twenty-seven yet. Did she really want to settle, no matter how sensible her choice? Looking at Clem's expression, she knew her sister was thinking the same thing.

'Rosy, I think this is something you need to take some time and think about.' Clem was obviously picking her words with care. 'Really think about. You need a break. Stay here for a few weeks, Rosy. You know the Cornish air does you good.'

Closing her eyes, Arrosa imagined waking up to the Cornish sun, long walks on the beach and carefree days. 'I'd love to, but I'm heading back tonight.' It had been hard enough concealing her movements for this one evening, any longer would be too dangerous.

'Tonight? Oh, Rosy. You said yourself that you have no meetings.'

'I don't, but the speculation if I'm not seen, even from a distance, could be damaging this close to the ratification. I didn't go anywhere for a couple of weeks when I had flu last year and, according to the tabloids, I was having a facelift, had joined a cult and eloped with a soldier.' She tried for a laugh, but she knew it was unconvincing and could see Clem's face crease with concern. 'I know it's silly and I shouldn't care, but it's not just that I don't want any rumours circulating at home— eventually the press would find me and then they'd start wondering who *you* are and that's the last thing you need. It's safest for you if we're not seen together, Clem.'

How she hated the subterfuge and lies, wished she and Clem could be sisters openly, but she had spent eight years being the target of press interest and speculation. There was no way she was subjecting her sister to that intrusion.

'*If* they find you. After all, why would they look for you here?' Clem paused, a thoughtful expression crossing her face. 'I could go back to Asturia in your place.'

*What* had she just said? Arrosa couldn't have heard her sister correctly. But Clem had a determined air that Arrosa recognised all too well, one that usually preceded a piece of mischief.

'You're serious? Clem, no one would *ever* think you were me.'

'Up close, no. But in the back of a car, hair all neat like yours, in your clothes, with those big sunglasses you wear? Why wouldn't they?

People see what they expect to see. We're the same build and height, the same colouring. And I'm an actress, I can walk like you, hold myself like you. You could have the summer here and I'll spend it in Asturia making sure the press gets enough glimpses to think you're busy preparing for the ratification and leaving you free to get some serious relaxation. I talk about my cousin all the time. No one here will think anything of it if we say I've got a job and you're cat-sitting. The only unbelievable part will be that I've been cast in anything. I'll have to claim I ended up on the cutting room floor.'

'That's the craziest thing I've ever heard. We'd never get away with it.' But how she wished they could.

'If you lived in the main castle or had dozens of servants then I agree, it would be impossible...'

'But I have my own cottage in the grounds of the Palais d'Artega,' Arrosa said slowly, the idea beginning to take shape. It was crazy and impossible, but she couldn't help imagining how it might work. 'People do come in to clean, but not when I'm around. Only Marie is there regularly, but of course she and Henri would need to know if there was any chance of this succeeding...'

*Was* there a chance? Clem was right, she had no appointments, no duties, no meetings for the next six weeks. No one was expecting to see her so who would know she wasn't actually there if Clem posed as her a couple of times a week in the back of a car? For a moment she allowed herself to visualise it, waking up to freedom, walks in public with no one taking any notice of her. But then reality inserted itself into her dreams. 'But it would be lonely, Clem. You'd have to be careful that no maids, no gardeners, no staff at all saw you. Some are new but some have been at the Palais since I was a baby. What would you do with yourself?'

'I'll make sure the press see Henri drive me around dressed as you, of course, but in between I'll wear my own clothes, let my hair go back to natural wildness and explore Asturia incognito. I've always wanted to go but somehow I never have. It would be a chance for me to see our father too. It'd be easier for him to spend time with me if I'm living at yours. No one would question him visiting you.'

Arrosa took another sip of wine and sat

back. Clem no longer sounded speculative or concerned—she sounded hopeful. Arrosa knew how much her sister longed for a real relationship with their father, more so since she'd lost her mother. Zorien was a politician and diplomat first, a family man second and Arrosa wasn't sure he would ever be what Clem wanted him to be, but her sister deserved the chance to find that out for herself. A few weeks living in Asturia, able to visit Zorien openly, might give her that opportunity.

Another objection occurred to her. 'But what's the point of me being here if you aren't?' Most of the joy of being in Cornwall was being with Clem.

'Well, Gus needs feeding for a start. The sea needs swimming in, scones need eating, beaches need walking on, and you need time to be you, not the Crown Princess and future Queen. This gives you that time. And I need a change of scene too. I've been putting off making plans for my future, just existing for too long. Maybe some time away will give me some much-needed perspective. You'd be doing me a favour.'

'Sure, *I'd* be doing *you* the favour.' Arrosa shook her head affectionately at Clem.

'We'll do each other a favour. We both need some time away from our lives, so why not swap for a while? Your mother's not at home, is she?'

'No, she's spending the summer on Ischia on a retreat.'

'Then we're safe. We could do this. Your call, Rosy. What will it be? Six weeks of avoiding Akil, ducking away from the press and worrying yourself into a shadow, or all the cream teas you can eat and a summer lazing on the beach?'

'We must be mad to even consider this would work.' But she couldn't deny she was tempted.

'It's easy enough to swap back if we need to,' Clem pointed out. Arrosa stared at her for another minute, unable to deny how sorely tempted she was. Not just tempted, she needed this, more than she wanted to admit. Why not agree and see what happened?

'You're right. Let's give it a week and see where we are. Thank you, Clem. Cornwall is just what I need, and I think maybe Asturia is where you need to be as well. To a change of scenery.' She held up her glass and Clem clinked it with hers.

'To the princess swap.'

# CHAPTER TWO

It took Arrosa several moments to realise where she was the next morning. So many nights she'd dreamt she was back in the Cornish cottage, it was almost a shock to find herself there in actuality and not just in her imagination. The cosy bedroom was exactly the same as it had been the last time she had slept here. It never failed to touch her that Simone and Clem had kept a room just for her. The imposing château in which she had been raised had never felt like home the way the cottage did, and even though at twenty-one she'd moved out to a villa in the estate grounds, when she thought of home she thought of here.

The walls were the same sea green she'd picked at fifteen, the curtains and bedspread the ones she'd chosen at the same time. The dressing table still held some out-of-date cosmetics and the hairbrush she'd left here eight years ago and the small built-in wardrobe was filled with her clothes, most of which still fitted despite being bought for a teen. She'd rifled through it nostalgically the night before, searching for pyjamas. Some of the clothes were a little out of date and some not suitable for a woman in her mid-twenties, but nobody would be photographing her here; there was no need to be the fashionable designer Princess who graced countless magazine covers. Here she could just be Rosy in a pair of shorts and bikini top. Besides, there was always Clem's room to raid if she needed anything more.

It wasn't just her room that had been preserved in time. Clem had left home at eighteen to go to drama school and her room, which had been redecorated the same time as Arrosa's, was still decorated in the grey and white with orange accents theme she'd chosen back then. As for Simone's room... A lump filled Arrosa's throat as she stood at the doorway. There was no trace of the sickroom it had become. Rather it was as if Simone would walk in at any time to pick up one of the chic scarves with which she would transform her deceptively simple clothes. Her jewellery hung from pegs on the wall, her bed heaped high with cushions, the window seat overlooking the sea dressed with her favourite cashmere throw. It was impossible to believe that she wouldn't be coming back.

It took Arrosa a couple of hours to get herself together and dressed, padding around the cottage as she reacquainted herself with every nook and cranny. She took coffee, fruit and yogurt outside to breakfast in the pretty cottage garden before donning some of her old denim shorts, teaming them with a bright pink vest top, tucking her curls into a ponytail and adding some sunglasses as she readied herself to leave the house.

Walking down the road, weaving in and out of crowds of tourists, browsing shop windows felt like a five-star luxury experience. Nobody was watching her, nobody was judging her, she didn't need to watch her facial expressions or ensure that every hair was in place. Almost unconsciously her stride lengthened, her pace got jauntier as she breathed in the fresh sea air and drank in the scenery. She was almost lost to her surroundings as she stepped into the road, only to stop with a shock as a car screeched to a halt, a heavy hand on the horn alerting her to the fact she had nearly got herself run over. Of course, they drove on the left here. Holding up her hands in apology, Arrosa stepped back, only to halt in surprise as she recognised the irate driver at the wheel. It was the man who'd spoken to her yesterday, Jack something. The one she'd told she wouldn't be sticking around, the one who had asked her out for a drink. Recognition mingled with interest and a pull deep down she barely recognised, a flare of attraction as she took in the broad shoulders, sensual mouth and hooded eyes.

Arrosa sensed the moment he recognised her in return, his expression changing from annoyed to momentary surprise to inscrutable. She flushed, realising that he must think that she'd lied to him to get out of the offered drink. To her surprise she felt a need to explain, to tell him that she had been tempted, surprisingly tempted, to accept, that she really hadn't expected to be here this morning. But as she stood there, hands outstretched in both apology and almost a plea to be heard, he nodded curtly before accelerating away.

'*Dammit,*' she muttered. But then again, what did it matter? It wasn't as if she'd see him again. But some of the jauntiness left her step as she continued her walk, looking out for traffic a little more carefully.

Attraction was almost a foreign feeling to her. She'd spent so long schooling her emotions to be the perfect princess, the perfect diplomat, that her own personal preferences were almost indiscernible even to her. It had been a long time since she'd had such an instinctive reaction to someone. It was nice in a way to know that she still could feel an instant attraction.

Remembering Clem's instructions to swim and eat, Arrosa popped into the bakery to buy some fresh scones, and then into the delicatessen to add jam, cream and strawberries to her bag, promising herself a jog, swim or both before she tucked in to the delicacies. As she left the deli she bumped into Clem's friend Sally who she'd known as a teen and, after explaining Clem's sudden absence and her own appearance, was delighted to be asked to come along to the pub on Saturday and invited to see the latest in a superhero series at the cinema with Sally and her daughter in a few days' time. The cinema usually meant formal premieres complete with red carpets and receptions and uncomfortable corseted ballgowns. The prospect of a normal seat with popcorn and company she'd chosen was enticing and she accepted with alacrity, promising to let Sally know about the evening drink as well.

Returning to the cottage with her bag bulging with local delicacies, Arrosa started to put them away, pausing to look at remembered plates and mugs, blinking back tears as she saw the jars of jams and chutneys labelled in Simone's exuberant script. She'd just started to chop up some salad for lunch when her phone pinged with a message and she picked it up, expecting to see Clem's name, only for embarrassment to surge through her when she saw Akil's name on the screen. Embarrassment and guilt; she couldn't believe she'd just run away from the awkward situation she'd put them both in. With no little trepidation she opened the message.

Arrosa, I'm at your house with Clem. Let me know everything is all right.

Biting her lip, she reread it. So much for her confidence that nobody would come seeking her and discover their subterfuge. Here they were, less than twenty-four hours after Clem had suggested swapping, and they'd already been found out. Did this mean that she would need to return home? With a heavy heart she tapped out a returning message.

Everything is absolutely fine. I just needed some space. You can trust Clem with anything.

Reading one of Simone's adored vintage crime books with lunch cleared her head somewhat, as did a run followed by a refreshing swim, and by the time she sat back down in the garden to catch the late afternoon sun, Gus at her feet, with a fresh cup of tea and her book some of the anxiety had faded. There was no need for Akil to tell anybody that Clem was in Asturia instead of Arrosa and she knew he was no gossip, that was one of the reasons she trusted him. But she couldn't help but be relieved when her phone rang and Clem's name lit up the screen.

'How's it going?' her sister asked.

'I've had a run, a swim and I've got a week's worth of calories waiting for me in the form of cream and buttered scones so I'm absolutely fine. I'm more worried about you. What happened with Akil?'

'He came to see you. It was all slightly mortifying. I couldn't pretend that I didn't know about your not-quite-a-proposal as he mistook me for you at a distance and by the time he realised I wasn't you he'd already mentioned it. In the end I didn't really have a choice, I had to tell him who I am. But don't worry, our secret's safe.'

Arrosa sat back, trying to decipher Clem's tone. There was a suppressed emotion she couldn't quite identify, a strange kind of self-consciousness, almost excitement, in her sister's voice. What *exactly* had she and Akil talked about?

'What did you think of him?'

'I liked him. I liked him a lot. Obviously, he's handsome, and he's clearly successful, but there's a lot more to him than that. You could do a lot worse, Arrosa.' Clem paused. 'But that's by the by. Being able to do worse is not enough. I still think you need more, you of all people, with the path you have to tread. You need a real partner, someone who loves you and will always put you first. And I told him so.'

Arrosa could just imagine it. Her sister was always forthright. 'What did he say?'

'He agreed that you both had a lot of thinking to do. But I'm going to say to you what I said to him: I can see why on paper you're a good match. You can trust him; he knows your world. But I think that if you focus on that rather than what's in your hearts then there'll be trouble down the line. You both deserve more than something second-best.'

Arrosa's eyebrows shot up. *Both* deserve more? It sounded as if Clem and Akil had had quite the chat. It also sounded as if Akil had made quite the impact on Clem. Interesting. But it was also reassuring to know that someone cared enough about her to be so blunt, to put her interests first. She might feel alone far too often, but she always had her sister.

'Look, Clem,' she said reluctantly. 'My assumption that nobody would come and visit me, that we could pull this off with no one the wiser, was obviously completely wrong. It's been one day and already you've had to explain who you are to someone. I feel better already, just having the chance to walk down the road without anybody knowing who I was is the tonic I needed. It gave me the space to untangle my head a little.' She blew out a deep breath and stared out at the sea in the distance, trying to crystallise her thoughts, rationalise her relief at being away, that odd jolt of attraction that reminded her that she was a woman as well as a princess.

'I think you're probably right,' she said slowly, feeling her way through her tangled thoughts. 'I suggested marriage to Akil out of fear and panic and they're not the right reasons for marriage. Who knows what the future holds? It'd be silly of me to close down any chance of a meaningful relationship just because I'm a little bit scared. So, job done, I feel better and I'm ready to call Akil and apologise for putting him in such an awkward situation. With all that in mind, maybe we should swap back.' She closed her eyes as she made the offer. It was the last thing she wanted, this tantalising hint of freedom to be lost before she'd really had a chance to enjoy it.

'You must be crazy,' Clem said emphatically. 'Unless you've gone around proposing marriage to several other suitable men, I can't see anyone else just turning up at a guarded palace without an invitation. Akil was clearly a special case. And no way is twenty-four hours enough time for you to be completely rested. And *I'm* not ready yet either. I've not seen our father and I've hardly started exploring. One trip to one beach and one lunch of clams, delicious as they were, isn't exactly the exploring I'd intended.'

'Which beach did you go to?'

'I'm not sure.' Self-consciousness entered Clem's voice. 'Akil took me out for lunch and for a walk.'

'That was nice of him.' The two had clearly hit it off. Arrosa wasn't sure what that meant but she resolved to clear the air—and clear up the situation—with Akil as soon as possible.

'Yes, it was. Look, Rosy, let's carry on for a little bit longer and see where we are. But I'm glad you're feeling better and I'm glad you've decided not to marry Akil. I really liked him and if you were in love with him would welcome him as a brother-in-law...' There was a tinge of reservation in her voice that Arrosa noted. Yup, Akil clearly had made *quite* the impression on Clem. 'But as you're not I really think it's for the best. And it's also for the best that you get a good long rest.'

'You're sure?' Relief flooded through Arrosa as she double-checked. It had been the right thing to offer to switch back but she didn't want to, not yet. If possible, she wanted the full six weeks. She wanted more scones, several trips to the cinema, to walk down the street every single day relishing her anonymity.

'I'm sure. Now, go eat that scone and don't

forget to send me a picture of Gus so I know you're remembering to feed him. Love you.'

'I love you too.' Arrosa ended the call and placed her phone back on the table, thinking about the next call she needed to make, and sooner rather than later. She might have more time but, before she could really enjoy it, she needed to clear things up with Akil. Not just for her own sake but for her sister's. The things Clem hadn't said were more telling than the things she had, and that self-consciousness in her voice was new.

Maybe she should suggest that Akil take Clem out for more sightseeing?

As for herself, if she saw Jack again she would apologise and offer to buy him a drink. It was the least she could do after misleading him, after all.

'Daddy, please come bodyboarding with us.' Clover tugged at Jack's hand and his phone nearly fell from his grasp, his email half drafted.

'Careful,' he said as he returned his attention to it. 'I need to finish this first. Why don't you carry on with your sandcastle?' He reread the carefully crafted words and added another line. It was time to pull in the big guns, get an external agency to advise on the comms strategy before his theatre plans were washed away by public disapproval.

'I finished my castle. Look, Daddy.'

The plaintive note in her voice tugged at his heart and Jack looked up to see Clover's disappointed expression, the familiar heavy feeling of guilt pressing down on him. He'd never really appreciated it before it had happened to him, the ever-present feeling of not being enough, not doing enough, that accompanied being a single parent. Not for the first time, and he knew not for the last, Jack wished he could go back in time and change all the careless things he'd said to his mother, the times he'd shown his own disappointment when he'd known full well that she was doing her best.

And that was all that anybody could ask, that he did his best. Which meant in this case heading into a crowded sea on a hot June weekend. 'Go on then,' he said, and Clover's bright smile was all the reward he needed. That was the thing about being six, tears turned to smiles in an instant. 'What about you, Tansy?' But he wasn't surprised when his eldest daughter shook her head, the long silky blonde hair and pointed chin so reminiscent of her mother it sometimes hurt to look at her, a reminder of his failures.

'I'll keep an eye on our things,' she said. 'Besides, I've got my reading list to finish.'

Jack touched her hair. 'You've been reading all morning. Come with us, your sister would love it.' But Tansy shook her head and returned to her book with a martyred air that was as worrying as it was irritating.

She'd always been a serious child, too serious her mother had said, with a sense of responsibility that seemed to negate her ability to just let go and have fun. But since Lily's death those traits had become more pronounced, a line of worry too often on her brow, a line wrong on an eleven-year-old girl. He caressed her hair again, telling himself not to mind as she shrugged him off with an exaggerated sigh.

'I'm *working*, Dad.'

'Okay, but you know where we are if you change your mind.' Jack looked back at the small erect figure, still worrying, as Clover pulled him into the cold waves. That was the thing about Cornwall. No matter how hot the outside temperature—and today was practically Mediterranean—the sea was always bracing. Clover didn't seem to notice as she hopped over waves, chattering on about her recent surfing lesson and how close she'd been to standing up. Some of the worry lifted as he listened. This was what he had brought them back here for, this kind of outdoor life, and the pink in her cheeks and happiness babbling through Clover's voice was all the affirmation he needed. Tansy would settle in soon enough.

As Jack and Clover waded in, waiting for the right wave to bodyboard into, he became aware of a slight figure standing further along, waist deep in the water. There was something about her that snagged his attention, the poised, graceful way she stood, almost regally, despite the surf pushing and pulling her. Jack noted dark wavy hair piled high, tendrils curling around a long neck, sunglasses shading high cheekbones. It was the woman from the theatre, the one he'd almost run into the other day. Rosy.

She wasn't moving, just standing still and letting the waves crash over her, but there was something about the way she looked up at the sky, the way she held her hands out that symbolised freedom. She looked as if she had been relieved of a huge burden and was taking this moment to celebrate with the elements. His mouth twisted wryly at the thought. It wasn't like him to be so fanciful, let alone weave stories around complete strangers—besides, she had told him that she wasn't staying around, she'd clearly wanted to let him down gently. He'd obviously imagined the strange instant connection that had seemed to sizzle between them.

As he stood and stared, Rosy turned slowly and her eyes locked on his for a breathless moment, a half-smile lingering on her full mouth before she held up one hand in a half wave. Jack nodded in return and then returned his attention to his daughter, trying his best to put the woman—Rosy—out of his mind.

The rest of the afternoon wasn't the success he'd hoped for when he'd suggested a beach day. It was hot, very hot, and the beach was crowded with the tourists who flocked to Polhallow during the summer months. As the day went on the noise on the beach grew, the sea crammed with swimmers and surfers, and Clover got first sand and then saltwater in her eyes. No sooner was that resolved than she started to cry because she was too hot, and then because she was hungry. Tansy read steadfastly on, pausing only to tend to her sister as if she were her mother, pulling first wet wipes and then suntan cream out of her bag.

'You can trust me to pack for us,' Jack said, half amused, half put out as his eldest daughter raised disbelieving eyebrows.

'Remember last time?' she said. 'You didn't remember Clover's juice.'

'That was different, I didn't expect it to be so hot last time.' And there it was again, that insidious feeling of guilt. He'd been back in Cornwall for over two months and this was only the second time he'd brought his girls to the beach—and the truth was he wouldn't be here now if the nanny hadn't broken her foot and returned to her parents for a few weeks. His daughters only had one parent. Providing for them wasn't enough, he had to make sure he met their emotional needs as well. He needed to play with them more—and somehow get Tansy to relax and trust him to have things under control.

Finally, he packed up their things, promising Clover an ice cream as they wended their way through the families, couples and groups of friends picnicking and lazing on the beach until they reached the beach café. A queue was snaking its way along the path and after a quick look at Clover's mutinous face Jack knew he would be there for some time. There was no way she was going any further without the promised ice cream and no amount of money or infamy would help him jump the queue. Forget the theatre, maybe he should buy an ice cream shop instead. He tried not to huff, jiggle impatiently or check his phone as they waited. Instead, he scanned the queue and, with that same feeling of almost inevitable recognition, clocked Rosy near the front.

Her hair was still tied up and she wore a long pink sundress over her bikini, a bag thrown over her shoulder, and yet she looked as cool and elegant as if she were in the middle of Paris, not on a hot sandy beach. As if aware of his gaze, she turned and looked at him, at Clover hopping from foot to foot and Tansy, who was sighing again as if Jack had conjured up the queue to annoy her, and waved, saying loudly and deliberately, 'Jack. *Jack*, I'm here!'

Both girls looked up at him in surprise. 'Who's that, Daddy?' Clover asked.

Jack squeezed her hand. 'Possibly the answer to our prayers. Just play along girls.'

Tansy said nothing but gave him a suspicious glance as Jack waved back and said extra heartily, 'There you are! I didn't see you, Rosy. Come on, girls. Let's tell Rosy what we want.' Nobody seemed to question the ruse as they joined Rosy at the front of the queue.

'Thank you,' Jack muttered with heartfelt gratitude and Rosy smiled radiantly, filling him with a warmth the situation hardly warranted. 'You've saved me from a long wait, which is no fun with overtired children.'

'It's no bother at all,' she said. 'Least I can do after stepping out in front of you the other day. I've been wanting to apologise. What can I get you—and, more importantly, what do the girls want?'

After some discussion, Clover decided on chocolate and Tansy vanilla with sprinkles.

'And you?' Rosy asked Jack.

He shrugged. 'I wasn't going to…'

'Daddy likes cherry,' Clover said, and Rosy's smile widened.

'Got it,' she said as she stepped up to the counter. She wouldn't take any money from him for the ice creams, insisting that it was her treat, and it seemed only polite that they fell into step with her as they walked away from the café.

'That was really kind of you,' Jack said. 'I think Clover was on the verge of a meltdown.

I probably kept her out too long. Tansy was right, as usual.'

'That happens a lot?'

'More and more since her mother died.'

'I'm sorry,' Rosy said, compassion in her eyes. 'That must be really hard for all of you.'

'It's been a couple of years, but there are still challenges. Right now, the nanny has broken her foot, so she's gone home to her family for a few weeks. The timing is difficult. We only moved back here recently so the girls haven't started school here yet and I have a lot to do. But I know how lucky I am to afford a nanny at all. I'll figure something out.'

'At least they have you. They're beautiful girls.'

'They take after their mother.'

Tansy and Clover had walked ahead and now they sat down on the sea wall to finish their ice creams and as Jack reached them and stopped, Rosy did too.

'Thank you for my ice cream,' Tansy said, and Clover echoed the thanks.

'You're very welcome. Actually, you did me a favour. Ice cream tastes better with company.' Rosy said.

'You decided to stay in Polhallow after all?'

Jack asked, and she shot him a slightly embarrassed grin.

'I wasn't lying,' she assured him. 'I had every intention of returning home after the play, but Clem got an unexpected job offer and needed someone to watch the house and feed the cat. I realised I could actually work from here for a few weeks, so here I am.' She shrugged a little self-consciously.

'That worked well for us. We'd still be in the queue now if it wasn't for you.'

'Where do you live?' Clover asked. 'We used to live in London, but Daddy moved here. Are you from London?'

Rosy shook her head. 'No, I come from a small country called Asturia, have you heard of it? Not many people have. But I came to school here in England, so I know London well.'

'I miss school,' Clover said.

'Ah, yes, your daddy said you haven't started school here yet. Are you looking forward to it?'

'Not really, mine is miles away.' Tansy glared at Jack.

It was an old argument, and not one Jack wanted to have in front of a stranger. 'It's a great school. You'll be fine. As we moved here just after Easter, I thought they might enjoy a long summer, especially as Tansy is starting secondary school. It didn't make sense sending her somewhere new for just one term,' he explained to Rosy. 'Tansy's school is about ten miles from here, and Clover is going to one the next town over.'

'Which means that not only do we not know anyone in Polhallow now, we won't know anyone here once we're at school either,' Tansy said.

'That's not true,' Jack said. 'There are children from Polhallow who go to both your new schools. You'll be fine.' He had the money to send the girls to the best schools possible and that was exactly what he was going to do.

'It can be tough to meet people when you move,' Rosy said sympathetically. 'But I know a little girl about your age,' she said to Clover. 'I'm going to the cinema with her and her mummy tomorrow in fact, to see that new superhero film. Do you want to come along and meet her?'

Clover's eyes widened as she turned to Jack imploringly. 'Can I, Daddy?'

'I don't know, honey.' He didn't know this woman beyond a jolt of attraction and a couple of random meetings. 'We wouldn't want to impose.'

'I'm sorry,' Rosy said, flushing. 'That was really clumsy of me. You don't even know me and here I am inviting your children out. I promise I'd take care of them. I can give you Sally's details—she's lived here all her life. Her little girl, Alice, goes to the local primary school and is Clover's age. I'm going to the cinema anyway; it really wouldn't be any trouble to take Clover as well—and Tansy if she would like to come.'

Jack hesitated. 'Sally Fletcher?'

'That's right, do you know her?'

'Only by sight. She was a few years younger than me at school, as was your cousin.' He must have seen Rosy around as a teen—but four years was a big gap at that age, and he'd left Polhallow when Sally and Clem had still been in their early teens. Still, the distant connection rooted Rosy, made her less a stranger. He looked at the girls and realised that not only was Clover looking hopeful but so was Tansy and his chest squeezed. She so seldom asked for anything. 'Are you sure it wouldn't be an imposition?'

'Not at all. In fact I haven't seen the first in the series so if the girls can bring me up to speed before the film starts, they'll be the ones doing me a favour.'

'Well, if you're sure...' The rest of the sentence was drowned out by Clover's yells of excitement and before he knew it they'd swapped numbers and Rosy made arrangements to collect the girls the following afternoon before walking off with a wave. Jack watched her retreat, admiring her elegant, graceful walk and feeling that same jolt of recognition and attraction she seemed to provoke in him every time they met. But one thing was sure, he would be checking in with Sally Fletcher tonight. Attraction or no attraction, he wasn't sending his girls out with a stranger. Their happiness and safety came first. Always.

# CHAPTER THREE

'ALICE IS REALLY nice, Daddy. Her mummy said that I can go over whenever I want. But I want her to come here and play in the treehouse. Can she, Daddy?'

Arrosa had barely had a chance to ring the doorbell before Jack had opened the door and Clover tumbled inside and onto him, babbling on excitedly about the afternoon's activities. Thank goodness she'd had such a good time; since yesterday afternoon Arrosa had asked herself several times what she'd been thinking of, volunteering to look after two complete strangers. Children at that! But once she'd collected them in Clem's small car her doubts had lessened then disappeared completely when they'd reached the cinema, where Clover and Alice had fastened onto each other like lifelong friends separated at birth, insisting on sharing their popcorn and sitting next to each other throughout the film and at the café they'd visited afterwards. However, Arrosa had been a little bit more concerned about Tansy and, despite their short acquaintance, that concern lingered.

There was something about the girl's preternatural maturity, the wrinkle of concern on her forehead, the way she watched her sister and fussed over her that made Arrosa's heart ache in recognition. She knew the signs all too well of a child who'd needed to grow up too fast, who'd shouldered responsibility beyond their years, but at least Arrosa had had summers here in Cornwall, a break from the rigid routine of her life, and her four years at boarding school to alleviate the pressure. Right now, she didn't see any sign that Tansy ever relaxed and, judging by the shadow lurking in Jack's eyes when he looked at his oldest girl, he too was worried.

At least Jack was aware; so many parents were oblivious to their children's struggles. Recognising them was the first step to solving them. Simone had taught her that and so much else that her own parents had been too busy to teach her.

Tansy followed her sister into the house, leaving Jack and Arrosa alone. Jack leaned on the door and smiled, his eyes filled with an approving warmth that seared through her. 'I'm sorry,' he said, holding the door a little bit further open. 'Where are my manners? Would you like to come in?'

She would like to, very much, but Arrosa held back. 'I'm sure you're busy,' she said. 'I'd hate to intrude.'

His eyes crinkled. 'You've given me the afternoon to work, I'm very appreciative. Please. Come in and have a coffee, it's the least I can offer in return. Are you sure they weren't too much trouble?'

'Not at all,' Arrosa assured him as she followed him into the wide two-storey hallway. She looked around with interest. She'd been impressed by the white nineteen-twenties Art Deco cube of a house with its stunning position on top of the cliffs when she'd driven up, but now she was inside she realised that the interior more than matched its outside. The house hadn't been clumsily extended or garishly modernised. Instead, it was as the architect had intended, spacious and graceful, the furniture chosen to complement the era but comfortable and obviously meant for a family to live with and use, rather than expensive antiques.

Arrosa had been brought up in a mediaeval château and spent many days in the imposing castle in the capital city where her father spent much of his time in the state apartments, and she had visited many of the heads of state around the world. She was used to money and she was used to luxury; she was used to historic and impressive buildings. Gorgeous as Jack's home was, it wasn't a palace, although money was clearly no object. But what struck her as she noted the carefully chosen art interspersed with framed children's pictures and family photos, the half open boot cupboard filled with sandals and wellies, the wicker basket stuffed with throws and cushions, was that this particular historic house was also a home. And that, as she knew all too well, was a much rarer combination.

'Nice house,' she said as she followed him into the kitchen. It was a huge room with views out towards the sea. The island in the middle held a jumble of paper, crayons and a half open book, the table by the French windows was already set for dinner. She swallowed. Jack Treloar was clearly a good father, embracing his children's clutter, not hiding it.

'We think so.' Jack leaned against the island and gestured for her to sit. 'I grew up here, in Polhallow, you know. I used to see this house and vowed one day it would be mine.' His mouth quirked into a self-deprecating grin. 'Some things should never be said out loud. That sounded like a line from a bad film. Apologies.'

'Not at all, it sounds impressive. How many people go on to achieve their dreams?' She didn't have dreams, didn't have anything to strive for. She just had duty. She envied him his purpose more than the achievement. Taking a seat at the island, she opted for a mint tea as Jack put the kettle on and took down two of the distinctive blue-striped Cornish mugs from the dresser. 'Thank you for loaning me your girls, they were great company. Alice and Clover definitely took to each other.'

Jack poured hot water into one of the mugs and handed it to her. 'That's good, they need friends. I didn't really think it through when I took them out of school after Easter. I just wanted to get them settled in before term started, give them a chance to have a long summer by the sea, to learn to surf and just enjoy being here. It's been a difficult couple of years since they lost their mother, I thought they could do with a break. But, of course, they are a little lonely. And, as you probably guessed, Tansy isn't keen on the school I chose. She wants to go to the local school.'

'That's where Clem went and where Simone taught,' Arrosa took a sip of the mint tea. 'I think it's a good one.'

'It is. But it's also the school I went to once upon a time.' He paused as he picked up his own mug. He didn't take a seat but resumed standing against the island, staring out to sea. 'I don't know if your cousin has mentioned me…'

'No, she hasn't. Besides, I don't like to gossip.' Although she *was* undeniably intrigued.

He laughed. 'Then you won't fit in around here. I've been the main topic of conversation in Polhallow for longer than I care to remember.'

'Either you have a very inflated sense of self-importance, or you really do have a reputation I should ask Clem about.'

'Probably both,' he said. 'The thing is, I don't really want my girls to know that side of my past. Not yet. I don't want them to overhear people talking about the theatre or raking up ancient history, gossiping about their mother. Besides, I've got the money, I can afford the best schools money can buy, so why shouldn't they attend them?'

Arrosa picked her words carefully, trying to dampen her interest. What past? She really *didn't* gossip but maybe she should check in with Clem. 'I don't think that my opinion matters here,' she said. 'You should do what's right for you, for your girls, not because of what anyone else says or thinks.'

His smile was rueful. 'A diplomatic answer. Forgive me, this is probably not what you expected when I asked you in for a drink. I seem to have forgotten how to do small talk—not that it was ever one of my skills.'

'I didn't have any expectations.' Arrosa picked up her mug again, glad of the distraction, but he was right. She'd expected a little bit of chitchat about the film, not this strange, intense conversation that felt almost as if they were jumping past the basics and getting straight to intimacy. But she couldn't let her guard down, not really. There was only so much that anyone could know about her. Not just because of her own need for anonymity but because Clem's identity was also at stake. Polite chitchat was all she could allow.

'Let's start again,' Jack said. 'So, what is

it you do when you're not housesitting for your cousin?'

'I'm a special adviser,' she said. It was almost true. She *did* do a lot of advising, trying to guide the politicians towards the policies she thought necessary for the development of her country. 'I work in diplomacy.'

Jack's eyebrows rose. 'Impressive. Do you offer lessons? Diplomacy is also something that doesn't come naturally to me.'

'Not to me either,' she confessed. 'I've had to learn.'

'And you can work from here, you said?'

'It's not usual, but as it's the summer I managed to make some arrangements. And I'm mostly taking the time off. It's been a long time since I was in Polhallow. I could do with a proper holiday and really get to know it again.'

'Any plans while you're here?'

'Actually, I am enjoying being plan free. I was a bit overstretched when I arrived, hence the time off. I had some tough decisions to make, so time and space is exactly what I need.'

'Personal or work?'

'Both, they get a little intermingled.' That was the understatement of the century. But at least she'd managed to step back enough to see that and to put right her misstep with Akil. She hadn't imagined the relief in his voice when she'd spoken to him a couple of days ago and suggested they stay friends and pretend her clumsy attempt at a proposal had never happened. She'd done her best to encourage him to see Clem again but hadn't heard anything since from either of them—which was either a really good sign or she'd completely misread the vibes she'd been getting from them.

'Tricky.'

She looked out at the view, as always, her anxiety abating at the sight of the sea. 'It is amazing what having the time and space to think does. Already I've made a really important decision and I feel so much better. But I really want to put work and home out of my mind and just enjoy being here—the only thing I want to worry about is the amount of clotted cream I'm consuming.'

He laughed then, warm and deep and toe-curlingly masculine. 'Yes, I'd forgotten how good food is here. London has every cuisine you can imagine but nothing tastes as good as Polhallow pastries and scones. If this carries on, I'll have to up my exercise time, which won't be easy with no nanny for the rest of the summer and all the work piling up.' He grimaced. 'Obviously, exercise is the least of my worries. This is a crucial time for the theatre renovation...' He slanted a quick glance in her direction as if waiting for a reaction. 'And my other businesses and interests need attention. But the girls can't just sit around and wait for me all day. I could try a temp agency to find a summer nanny, but they've been through so much change I don't want to risk a mismatch.'

'I could watch them sometimes,' she offered impulsively. It wasn't just that she had the time, although she did, something about Tansy still bothered her, even though she could see what a safe and loving home the girl had. She understood what it was like to feel responsibilities at a young age in a way that not many other people did. She also knew how important it was to let those responsibilities go and to have fun. Maybe she wouldn't be able to make any difference to the girl's life, but Arrosa felt an overwhelming urge to try.

It didn't hurt that she was enjoying spending time with Jack either, that she was all too aware of his every shift and movement, how the light moved across the planes of his face, the way his eyes darkened to navy when he was moved, the shape of his mouth.

'I can't ask you to do that!' But she could see he was tempted, relief clearing some of the cloud from his expression.

'You didn't. I'm not offering to be a stand-in nanny, I'm not at all qualified and I *am* on holiday. But I would be more than happy to take them around a little bit, go to the beach, organise some play dates with Sally, go to the cinema—they'd be a great excuse for catching up on all the summer releases.'

'I am really tempted…' At the word their gazes caught and locked, and she felt again that odd sense of knowing him, feeling the attraction building between them, unlike anything she'd experienced on so short an acquaintance—or even a longer acquaintance—before. 'But I'd be totally taking advantage of your good nature.'

'We could take it on a day-by-day basis. If I have free time and you need a hand then great, but I will be absolutely comfortable saying no if I have plans, and if you decide you need something more structured I won't be offended.'

'It sounds too good to be true. Look. Before you make a decision you should see them at their overtired worst. Stay for dinner and if at the end of it the offer is still open we'll discuss payment and other issues then.'

Arrosa would of course turn down the offer of payment, she had no need of money. But nobody had ever offered to pay her before. She had an allowance—a generous allowance— but it wasn't a salary. It was nice to be thought worth a wage.

She had no idea what Jack did but he was clearly well-off. It was obvious from the house and furnishings, in the way he dressed, even in a casual linen shirt and jeans, both top quality and fitting as if made for him, the linen almost—tantalisingly—translucent, the jeans clinging to narrow hips and strong, lean thighs. She swallowed, mouth dry.

'What's for dinner?'

'Lasagne. I've only got a few dishes in my repertoire and lasagne is near the top.'

'With salad and garlic bread?'

'Of course!''

'That sounds delicious. Thank you, I'd love to have dinner with you.'

But as she sat down and accepted the glass of white wine he handed her, Arrosa couldn't help wondering if she was completely mad.

She should be heading out of the door as fast as she could go, not offering to babysit Jack's children. She might be inexperienced with relationships in the real world but even she could feel the chemistry sizzling between them. She was a princess, and he was a widower with two small girls. Neither should indulge in summer flirtations, no matter how tempting.

But, on the other hand, she had promised herself a summer off. A summer of being just Rosy. This was just dinner—and a dinner chaperoned by his daughters. What harm could one evening do?

As June continued the British summer started to live up to its flaky reputation. The long, hot early summer days had been replaced by intermittent rain and drizzle, interspersed with moments of blazing sunshine. It was the kind of weather that meant leaving the house without a bag packed with suntan cream, wellies, sunhats and raincoats was ill-advised. Jack was seriously considering investing in a mule to help with the baggage even a brief walk entailed. Worse, the weather made entertaining the girls even more tricky and he couldn't help but think his decision to give them an extra-long summer had been ill thought through: weeks filled with adventure and time to explore was idyllic on paper but, in reality, less than practical, especially now he was looking after them alone.

This was where being a single parent was so hard. There was nobody to sense check his ideas with. But, then again, Lily had always preferred to leave all responsibility to him. She would probably have enthusiastically supported the thought of a long summer, come up with a dozen impractical plans and whipped the girls up into a frenzy of expectation before disappearing off for a summer of house parties and social events, leaving the girls to their nanny. As for the autumn, she would have wanted Tansy away at boarding school, not at a private day school just a few towns over. After all, she'd first suggested sending her when their eldest had been barely eight. He could hear her now, those languid upper-class tones caressing and yet repelling him at the same time.

*'But darling, girls of that age are tricky. I should know!'* Tinkling laugh. *'She'd be much happier with girls of her own age, don't you think?'*

No, he would have got no backup or sense

checking from Lily. It had always been down to him where the girls were concerned. So why was he suddenly feeling so lonely—and second-guessing himself? Maybe it was because Tansy was entering those dangerous tween and teen years and he of all people knew how important stability was around then, especially for those whose early years had been the opposite. His childhood had, despite his mother's best endeavours, been difficult and his early teen years full of trouble and mischief; he'd come very close to getting a criminal record. But then again Lily had had everything and she had thought herself invincible, had adored the thrill of danger. That was why she had taken up with him after all—there was nothing as rebellious as dating the village bad boy. Getting pregnant and marrying him had been the ultimate rejection of all her parents' hopes for her.

Lily had loved her girls—but she'd been impulsive and heedless, and Tansy especially had been painfully aware of how mercurial her mother could be. Her death had obviously compounded Tansy's insecurity and, although she was less than enthusiastic about the move, part of his motivation for returning to Cornwall was to try and centre her somewhere less frantic and fast paced than the big city.

'Come on, girls,' he said for the twentieth time that day. The words were fast becoming his catchphrase, maybe he should get them tattooed on his forehead. As usual they had little effect as Clover dawdled behind in a world of her own, Tansy walking in the middle, looking most put upon. But, to be fair, he knew that a business meeting was not their idea of a fun afternoon out, even if it *was* in a theatre.

Of course, he could have taken Rosy up on her offer to watch them sometimes. It had clearly been genuinely meant. She seemed to like the girls and, more importantly, they clearly liked her. But he'd been reluctant to get back in touch with her after the evening they'd spent together. Not because he hadn't enjoyed it. In fact, quite the opposite. The whole evening had gone smoothly, with conversation and laughter flowing easily. She fitted in with them, almost too well, and by the end of dinner the girls were acting as if they'd known her all their lives. But they *didn't* know her. He had no real idea where she was from, what she did or how long she would stay. And the last point was crucial.

Clover was predisposed to like everybody, but his eldest was a different matter and Rosy and she seemed to have connected. He hadn't heard Tansy chat so much or laugh so much or volunteer so much information in a long time. Which was why he hadn't dared ask Rosy to watch then—she was only here for the summer. He couldn't risk his girls getting too attached.

Or himself. The attraction he felt had just intensified with the time they'd spent together but he couldn't allow himself the indulgence of a fling.

'Rosy!'

Jack looked up in surprise as Clover's cry interrupted his thoughts. There, as if he'd summoned her by thought alone, was Rosy, casually dressed in jeans, a turquoise T-shirt and a long grey cardigan, but yet again something about the way she wore the simple outfit elevated it to a high fashion statement.

Rosy's face lit up. 'Hello, how are you two? I was just thinking about you.' And then, more quietly, 'Hi, Jack.'

'Hi.' For a moment they both just stood and looked at each other, Jack almost lost in her hazel eyes, a beguiling mix of green and amber, in the warmth of her smile.

'You were? Why?' Clover danced up to Rosy and tugged at her hand. 'Why were you thinking about us?'

'I had a surfing lesson this morning with Dan, and he said that you are both naturals. Unfortunately, he didn't say the same about me. Which is very lowering because once upon a time I was not bad at all. Take my advice, girls; don't stop for years or you'll lose all your balance and skill.' She mock sighed and both girls giggled. 'Where are you off to? Somewhere fun?'

'We're going to the theatre,' Clover told her. 'Daddy has a boring meeting.'

'Boring? The theatre? Surely not. There's a stage and an auditorium, lots of fun places to discover. Do either of you like plays?'

'I do,' Tansy said. 'Drama was my best subject at school. I should have had the lead in the end of term play, but we moved.' She gulped and blinked rapidly, eyes reddening as Jack stared at her in consternation. He knew that Tansy liked acting but in his haste to leave London he hadn't even considered the end of term play which was the highlight for year six leavers. But he should have—after all, Tansy had been fixated on starring in it ever since she'd started school.

'They put on plays in the theatre and local people can be in them,' Rosy said, to Jack's relief. 'That's where my cousin Clem started and now she's a professional actress. I'm sure she'd be happy to talk to you about it and give you tips.'

'Do you really think so?'

'I know so. She's always happy to chat acting and plays—and I bet she could introduce you to the community theatre group if your dad didn't mind.'

'That would be brilliant.' All trace of tears had gone as Tansy turned to him. 'Can I, Dad?'

'It sounds good, let me look into it.' He needed to bring the community theatre onside first. The last thing he wanted was for Tansy to be ostracised because of him.

'Come with us to the theatre?' Clover asked Rosy and Tansy agreed.

'Please do, it'll be a lot more fun if you're there.'

'Thanks, girls!' Jack laid a firm hand on both blonde heads. 'I'm sure Rosy has better things to do than tag along to my business meeting.'

But Rosy didn't take the get-out clause he'd handed her. 'Actually, if you don't mind, I'd like to come. I haven't looked around the theatre properly for years. My aunt—Simone Beaumont—the theatre was her pet project. The first time I came here to stay she spent the whole summer writing out grant applications and organising fundraising events. When they reopened it after the renovations the councillor who gave a speech said that she had single-handedly saved it. They were going to demolish it originally. Simone had many causes and projects, but this theatre was her main passion—sometimes I wonder if that's why Clem took up drama, so her mother could see her on this stage. Simone could be a very busy woman. It was hard to pin her down, but she never missed a single performance.'

Jack shot Rosy a sharp glance, but she was all innocence. Maybe she had no idea of his plans. If not, if he could show her his vision then maybe she would be able to convince her cousin that he was on the village's side? 'In that case of course you're welcome to come along.'

In the end he found that he was relieved to have Rosy with him as he sat down with the PR agency he was considering hiring. Investing in the theatre was so unlike anything he had ever done before. He knew he needed guidance. He was usually the man behind the scenes, the angel investor being wowed not doing the wowing, listening to PR teams not recruiting them. It was important he brief the company well. But as he expanded on his vision he could see the girls and Rosy exploring, hear laughter and chatter coming from all areas before the three ended up on the stage, clearly putting on some kind of mini play, Tansy directing the other two.

Jack paused and watched the antics on stage. It was so good to see Tansy acting her age, he needed to ensure it happened more often. Maybe he should stop worrying about what would happen when Rosy left and take her up on her offer to watch his daughters. It would be good for the girls.

As for him, he might be attracted to her but that didn't mean he needed to act on it.

Finally, the meeting came to an end and after taking some photos the agency representatives left, leaving Jack alone at the top of the auditorium answering some emails. A slight sound made him look up to see Rosy making her way across the row to join him. The girls were still on stage, volubly discussing who should be standing where.

'Exhausted by artistic endeavours?'

Dimples flashed. 'I'm not the actor, that's Clem. Tansy definitely needs to meet her. That daughter of yours has got some real understanding of staging.'

'Never been tempted to do something that way yourself?'

'Not at all.' She laughed a little self-consciously. 'Acting has never been a love of mine. I was more likely to be found painting scenery than trying out for the lead. But in some ways, I guess, I do spend a lot of time acting, channelling a more confident, assertive me. Clem taught me techniques—how to stand, to project. How to breathe—that's been very useful. Simone was great too at preparing me to speak up in intimidating circumstances. She was one of the most matter-of-fact and forthright people you'll ever meet, she passed that quality onto Clem. They both taught me to focus on what's important. I owe them both a lot.'

'Sounds like being a diplomat is hard. You must be young to have so much responsibility. I think of diplomats as older—not that I've dedicated too much time to the topic,' he added hastily, although he had been thinking about it of late, since meeting her.

'I *am* young to have some of the responsibilities I do, but politics is the family business. I was raised to it. And yes, at times the focus is on me, but more what I represent, if that makes sense, rather than me as a person. That's why it can help to play a part, to take the personal out. How about you? What's today about? Planning to set up a troupe of players to stage your opus?'

'Not exactly. I'm not one for being on stage either, but I am interested in this theatre in particular.'

'In what way?'

He took a deep breath. Now was the time to make his pitch. 'I want to take out a long-term lease and carry on the restoration process to take the theatre to the next level. Make it an asset that *works* for the community, *not* take it away from the community.' He could hear his tone sharpen at the last words and her eyes widened.

'You clearly feel passionately about it,' she said.

Jack nodded grimly. 'I'm not the only one. According to the village—and your cousin—everything I want to do goes against what this theatre is for. That's what the meeting just then was about—I am going to have to hire a

PR firm to untangle the web of gossip and rumours about what I am trying to do here. Because it *will* happen. The Council will lease it to me, they have to. This place is expensive to run, they're relieved to get it off their hands, for someone else to be responsible for the upkeep, but I'd rather go ahead with the backing of the village. I'm not interested in cementing my role as the bad boy outsider.'

Rosy sat back, eyebrows raised. 'Is that who you are? That's not how I would describe you. A hard-working father maybe, a mean maker of a lasagne, a man who obviously cares about his community, but not a bad boy outsider. And I'm usually a good judge of character.'

Her words warmed Jack through. Maybe he did have a chance to start again—with the incomers at least. 'People in Polhallow have long memories and the Treloars a certain reputation. I wouldn't care if it wasn't for the girls.' He stopped and thought about his words. 'That's not true. I do mind, I always have,' he admitted, surprised at his honesty, to her and to himself. 'But back then, instead of trying to prove people wrong, I went the other way, became the boy they expected me to be for a short while. But even when things changed, when *I* changed, all the local community could see was who they expected to see. And that is who many people in the village see now, no matter where I live or how I act. They hear I have plans for the theatre and assume the worst because of my name and the actions of a messed-up teen. That's not what I want for the girls. I want people to hear their name and respect them, respect their origins.'

'That seems like a laudable ambition to me,' she said softly and with her words he felt some of the brittleness within him break as if she had given him a benediction, a blessing on his plans.

'You want to hear what I have in mind?'

Rosy reached out and touched his arm, the warmth of her touch searing him. 'I'd love to.'

'Come on then.' This was a great opportunity to start to change things. Clem was influential and if her own cousin could advocate for him then his battle might be half won before it started. But as Jack began to expand on his ideas, he knew that it wasn't the village he was trying to impress—it was this one woman.

# CHAPTER FOUR

ARROSA WASN'T JUST being polite when she said she wanted to hear more, although it was Jack's allusions to his youthful reputation and motivations that piqued her interest rather than the actual means of achieving his aims. But as the tour progressed she got swept away. There was something about Jack's vision that made things come alive. She could see the theatre as he did, filled with chattering, excited people, smell the greasepaint, feel the heat of the lights. She could see the entrance opened up and welcoming, imagine the glass-fronted café overlooking the bay, picture the currently unused boxes turned into sought-after seats for special occasions. He didn't just want to restore the front of the theatre, he also had plans to refurbish the dressing rooms, currently more reminiscent of a school locker room, and create VIP areas backstage.

'I want to attract the best,' he told her as he sketched out his ideas. 'The best dance companies, opera, repertory theatre, touring musicals, even bands. When I was a kid we had to travel for any kind of culture, which for people like me meant it was completely inaccessible. When Lily and I moved to London I was intimidated by theatres and museums, I didn't think they were for the likes of me. I don't want any child within twenty miles of here to ever think that. I want this to be a destination theatre that attracts tourists all year round, but it's important that anyone and everyone who lives here has full access too—and at an affordable price. What do you think?'

Arrosa circled round, seeing the currently drab bar area through his eyes, bright and busy. 'Honestly? I love it! Your plans are completely inspiring.' She meant every word although she knew Clem was opposed to any changes to the current set-up. But surely her sister wasn't fully informed about what Jack had planned? Loyalty to Simone might make Clem stubborn but her own ambitions for the theatre weren't dissimilar to everything Jack wanted to do. 'But I can see your comms problem; I've not heard anything about any of this, just that the theatre needs saving.'

'I think I went about it all wrong, dived straight in without laying the groundwork first.' Jack was clearly frustrated. 'I'm not used to being the upfront spokesperson, I'm usually behind the scenes. I thought the plans would speak for themselves, but as soon as it became known I wanted a long lease and changes were involved rumours started. You can see why I need a PR agency to help turn things around.'

'Changing public perceptions can be a long process and it's important to remember that even if opposition feels personal it usually isn't,' she assured him. She should know. After all, it had been over eight years since realising his hoped-for son was never going to come, her father had turned his attention to amending Asturia's laws in order to make Arrosa Crown Princess and eventual Queen. They'd had to work tirelessly over those eight years to get to the point where public opinion was in favour and for all the opposition parties to agree to change the age-old laws. Eight years of Arrosa not putting a foot wrong, of treading the delicate line of not looking too eager to become Queen whilst displaying leadership and diplomacy. Eight years of only being photographed looking calm, friendly and professional.

Eight years of knowing that this was just the beginning. That her entire life had to live up to the promise of her eight year-long audition for the role.

'Daddy, I'm hungry!' Clover clambered up the stairs towards them. 'Can Rosy have dinner with us again?'

Arrosa could see Jack hesitate and tried to think of an excuse she could use to help him out as after an uncomfortable pause he nodded. 'Of course. She's very welcome if she doesn't have other plans.'

'I did defrost a chicken.' It was a rubbish excuse, and she knew it from the disappointment in Clover's face. 'But you could come to me,' Arrosa offered before she could remember all the reasons getting further entangled with the small family was a bad idea.

Jack didn't reply at once. Instead, he met her gaze as if seeking confirmation that the offer was genuine and not mere politeness. Not for the first time, Arrosa noted the wariness behind what often looked like arrogance and confidence, giving her a sense of the lonely and potentially misunderstood boy he had once been. 'If you're sure. There's a lot of us to feed.'

'I can't promise anything as magnificent as your lasagne,' she said. 'But I could cook you chicken the Asturian way with lemon and garlic, fresh salad and these little cubed potatoes covered with a special secret spicy sauce. Does that sound any good?'

Clover agreed volubly that it did and before Arrosa knew it she was being whisked back home in Jack's oversized car, despite protesting it was only a short walk away. He parked outside and she opened the little picket gate, the family following her down the path which wound through the flower-filled garden to the white cottage's front door.

'Is this your home?' Clover asked as Arrosa unlocked the front door and ushered them inside.

'No, it belongs to my cousin Clem, but it *feels* like my home. I spent lots of very happy times here.'

The cottage was very old, parts of it dating back to Elizabethan times, with a large hallway which held a cupboard for coats and shoes, a hatstand and a table flanked by small chairs. Doors on either side led into low-ceilinged square rooms, on the left the sitting room, on the other a combined library, study and dining space. This was the room where Simone had often held court, plotting out her many campaigns, the dining table more often used to paint placards than to hold food.

The kitchen ran across the whole back of the cottage, holding at one end a battered leather sofa and an ancient pine kitchen table, with wooden cabinets painted a pretty eggshell blue and worktops on the other side. Stairs led up from the kitchen to the three bedrooms and one bathroom. It was simple but, thanks to Polhallow's popularity as a holiday destination and desirability as a second home location, Rosy knew the house would sell for a small fortune—but nowhere near the amount of money Jack's stylish white cube would command.

There were colourful paintings and framed posters on every available wall space and photos on every table and shelf. Jack wandered over to examine a collection of photos on the kitchen dresser, mostly Clem in various roles. Some were of Simone, often with a placard in her hand, off to save whatever cause she was spearheading that month, but there were also photos of her as a young woman, of the chic student who had attracted a future king, of the backpacker on the deck of a boat, of the young mother with her arms around a tiny Clem. There were no pictures of Arrosa on public display, it was too dangerous in case anyone recognised her, but she knew that upstairs on Simone's bedside table a photo of Arrosa and Clem side by side had pride of place.

'Your aunt taught me at school,' Jack said after a while. 'She was always kind. Bracing, said what she thought, but kind.'

Arrosa laughed. 'Those traits run in the family; Clem is just the same.'

'In your family too?'

Arrosa thought about her father, always King first and second, father a poor third. Of her mother, whose feelings were always hidden behind a regal smile. 'They are diplomats, as you know,' she said. 'It's an innate characteristic, even at home.'

'Sounds chilly.'

Chilly. Was that the right word? Formal, yes. But not cold exactly. 'Their expectations of me are high, that's true. That's why I liked being here, where the only expectations were that Clem and I help out making placards, or working bake sales, or one unforgettable summer trying to knit squares for a peace blanket, although it turned out knitting wasn't something either of us were good at! Simone was a second mother to me.'

'You were lucky to have her,' Jack said, and she nodded.

'Lots of people felt the same way—that Simone was like an aunt or a sister. She had a gift of drawing people in. That's part of your problem with the theatre. I think people feel that your plans might expunge what she did. It wouldn't even still be here without her, they were going to knock it down, as you know, and she spearheaded the campaign to keep it and raised the money to restore it. But, actually, I can't help thinking that she would be excited by your ideas.'

'You think?' His rather grim expression relaxed and Arrosa felt her stomach flip.

'The problem is your timing is off. Simone is so recently gone; Clem is still grieving. I think that's why she and the rest of the community group jumped straight into organising a campaign against you. Simone loved a campaign. It's a way of keeping her close, especially as they feel your plans are a threat to her legacy. You need to listen to their concerns and show them that you need their expertise and passion, want them involved, that this is an evolution not a takeover. It might help to acknowledge the original restoration campaign in all your literature and plans, name some part of it after Simone.'

Jack didn't reply at first, his face thoughtful. 'You're right of course. Thank you,' he said after a while.

'An outsider's perspective is always useful.'

'No, it's more than that. I can tell you're used to brokering deals. Treaties must fall into your hands.'

'I wouldn't quite say that.'

'You've given me a lot to think about. Thank you.' He picked up a photo of Simone standing outside the theatre, grinning widely. 'If you wouldn't mind, I'd love your input when the PR agency send me their campaign ideas. You have a real insight; your thoughts would be invaluable.'

'You're welcome.' Arrosa could feel her face flush at the unaccustomed thanks. In her job nobody ever said *well done*, there were no performance reviews, apart from tabloid headlines, newspaper articles or social media posts as likely to be sharply critical as they were to be fawning. It might be silly to feel quite so touched by a few words of praise, but she was.

It didn't take her long to rustle up dinner, setting the kitchen table with the pretty floral dinner set that Simone had bought from a car boot sale many years before and the antique pearl-handled cutlery Arrosa had given her one birthday.

'I love this house, it's like a fairy tale cottage,' Clover said as they sat round the table after dinner, an old edition of Snakes and Ladders in front of them.

'It is, isn't it? I felt very lucky to spend my summers here,' Arrosa agreed.

'What's your own home like? Did you live somewhere like this when you were little?' Tansy asked.

Arrosa paused and thought. How could she convey the difference between the small, comfortable, chic yet homey cottage and the vast palace filled with antiques and portraits of ancestors where she'd been raised without giving away anything about who she was? Of course she'd had acres of land to run and ride on, a lake to swim in, woods to build dens in, but it had all been rather lonely. Her ancestral estate might have been a more fun place to grow up if she'd had a sibling who lived with her rather than one a thousand miles away.

'Not really. I'm an only child, you see.'

Every time she said that it felt like a betrayal of Clem. 'My parents are diplomats, so we always lived in houses that weren't exactly ours.'

That wasn't a lie. The family estate and the castle, where her father resided most of the time in state apartments, belonged to the country, not to Arrosa or her family. They were owned by the crown, her family were custodians not owners.

'A lot of the furniture was antique, so we had to look after it,' she continued. 'I can't complain, I've been very lucky. I've travelled a lot and I've met some important people, and I've seen many, many things that I wouldn't have if I'd lived a different life, but the truth is when I think of home this cottage is the place I see. I'm just glad I get to spend the summer here. That this is where I spent many happy childhood summers.'

Tansy shook the dice and gleefully moved her counter up a long ladder to Clover's voluble dismay. 'Polhallow is so small though. Didn't you get bored spending every summer here?'

'*Bored?* Never.' Arrosa got up to collect the cake she'd bought from Sally's family's café earlier, cutting generous slices and placing them on the table. 'Sometimes, Tansy, you have to find your own adventures. I suppose I was a little bit older than you when Clem and I started to go out by ourselves, but there was always something to do. Surfing, of course, swimming, going for ice creams, learning to sail. But simpler things too. For instance, we built our own adventure trail once in the woods outside the house and we used to camp out in the garden sometimes; one summer it was so hot I don't think we slept indoors for a month. We even tried to persuade Simone to let us build an outdoor loo and shower, but she resisted. Although I think that was more Clem than me. I was actually quite relieved to be able to go in and use a proper bath.'

'Camping! I've never been camping.' Tansy turned to her father. 'Daddy, can we get a tent? Can we sleep in the garden like Clem and Rosy did? I've always wanted to try.'

Jack reached out for his cake with a nod of thanks. 'Tansy Treloar, you have been on some incredible holidays. How many theme parks have you been to? And that amazing resort in Sardinia with five swimming pools where you got to do activities all the time. Would you really rather sleep in a tent?'

'It would be fantastic,' she said, eyes shining, and Clover joined in.

'Please, Daddy! I've always wanted to sleep in a tent too, always!'

Arrosa couldn't help but laugh. 'It's a long time since I've camped,' she said. 'And it can be amazing, but don't get carried away. It can be hard to get the balance of blankets right. One moment you're boiling hot, the next you're freezing cold, and then, of course, if you need the loo in the middle of the night you have to walk across the dew-filled field to get to it and if you forget wellies that means soggy feet. Sometimes spiders and other creepy-crawlies can find their way into the tent, but on the other hand, there is something special about sitting around a campfire and looking up at the stars and telling each other stories. Toasting marshmallows, of course.'

Oh, dear. Both girls' eyes had grown bigger and their expressions more excited, but Jack's lips were compressed. She probably shouldn't have said anything. 'But five swimming pools in Sardinia sounds pretty amazing too. And you guys have a swimming pool at your house too. If Clem and I had had a pool of our own I'm sure that would have kept us busy.'

Her attempt to backtrack obviously hadn't helped. Tansy turned to Jack, her face full of hope, her voice pleading. 'Daddy, *please* can we go camping?'

'Sorry, Tansy, but absolutely not.' He sounded adamant.

'But…'

'I said no. The subject is closed.'

Arrosa stared at Jack in surprise. He seemed like a very capable man to her. He was physically fit, and the lean muscles she was all too aware of didn't seem like gym-built bulk but rather the muscles of a man who was prepared to put his hand to anything that needed to get done. He'd been raised around here, a local boy, which meant he was likely to be outdoorsy. Surely a couple of nights in a tent wouldn't be that big a deal?

He caught her eye and she sensed that he knew what she was thinking.

'It's after six,' she said. 'Do you want a beer? You can walk back from here. And girls? How about I make you hot chocolate with marshmallows and we can take it outside and sit around the fire pit?'

The suggestion was met with approval and Arrosa got herself and Jack a beer, sending the girls out to gather some firewood from the

log pile with strict instructions not to go anywhere near the matches until she was there,
and showed them how to lay and light a fire
properly.

'Simone got a fire pit long before it was
fashionable, thanks to Clem and my obses-
sion with being outside in all weathers,' she
said as she spooned hot chocolate into mugs.
She reached into the cupboard for the marshmallows. 'I'm sorry, I didn't mean to get the
girls so excited.'

She dropped a handful of marshmallows into each cup and added hot water before carrying the tall mugs over to the table.
'Parenting must be hard enough without well-
meaning outsiders stirring things up.'

Jack reached up and took one of the mugs
from her and put it down, knowing he owed
Rosy an explanation at the very least. 'Look,
I'm the one who should apologise. That was
a bit of an overreaction.' He winced. 'I seem
to have fallen into a pattern of promising to
be a better father and then messing up at the
first opportunity.'

Rosy set the mug she was holding down
and pulled at a chair. 'Don't be silly. I completely understand. Now I'm an adult, I'm

all about the thread count and a good mattress too.'

Jack exhaled slowly. He could, he should, leave it there. Let her believe he just didn't want to rough it, that money had turned him into the kind of man who needed five-star service and all the trimmings. But he wanted her to think better of him. Needed her understanding in a way he couldn't articulate.

'It's not that. I wish it were that simple.'

She pushed a curl behind her ear. 'Jack, you don't owe me any kind of explanation. Whatever your reasons, I'm sure they're valid, but it's really none of my business.'

'As I mentioned earlier, the Treloar name isn't particularly respected around here. My father, my grandfather, even my great-great-grandfather, were petty thieves, petty criminals, lazy vagabonds all. Go through the village's history and you'll find our name over and over, mentioned for public drunkenness, begging, theft. My mother was the complete opposite. She was—is—hardworking and no-nonsense, but she came down here on holiday and fell for my father's charms, such as they were, and stayed. I don't think it was long before she realised what a bad bargain she had made when she was left alone with me, working three jobs to try and keep food on the table and a roof over our heads.'

'She sounds like quite a woman.'

He nodded. 'She is. Not an easy woman. Life made sure of that, knocked the warmth and trust out of her early, but she is everything my father wasn't. And she did her best by me.'

'That's all any of us can ask.'

He nodded. 'She was always determined that, no matter how bad things were, we would have a holiday. Now I'm an adult I can see she needed to get away herself, leave her life behind for a few days, go somewhere where she wasn't pitied or looked down upon.'

'That's understandable.'

'Of course all we could afford was to camp. She didn't have a car so we would take the bus and carry everything. We couldn't go too far because it would be expensive, so usually we made it just over the border into Devon. And then we would find the most basic, cheapest campsite we could, set up our tent and live on baked beans and sausages, cooked over the fire, marshmallows as a treat.'

He could almost smell the sausages, hear the crackle of the fire and, despite himself, his mouth curled into a reminiscent smile.

'Looking back, those were some of the happiest times we shared. She was usually too busy to spend much time with me, but those camping weeks we were together all the time. But with such limited resources we couldn't do much other than walk, swim or hang out reading at the campsite. Probably exactly what she needed, but the older I got, the more I realised how different my holiday experience was to other kids'. One year she was getting the tent out and I told her not to bother. That I hated holidays with her. Why couldn't we go on a proper holiday like normal people?' He inhaled, the old shame filling him. 'I'll never forget the stricken expression in her eyes. She didn't say anything, just put the tent away and we never went camping again. I'd give anything to go back and change that day, give anything to help her get the tent ready.'

'Jack, I'm sure she knew you didn't mean it, not really.'

'But that's just it. I *did* mean it and she knew it. Oh, I have apologised since, many times. But I hurt her dreadfully that day, not just with words but with my contempt and carelessness, like my father before me.'

His behaviour still shamed him. The memory shamed him. As it should.

'Does she still live around here?'

'She moved to Spain a few years ago.' He'd offered her an allowance but she'd turned it down, so instead he'd funded the purchase of a beach bar and bought her a comfortable villa. 'We have a good relationship now when we see each other, but I caused her a lot of anxiety when I was younger, and I'd give anything to take it back. Sometimes it feels as if those camping holidays sum up my childhood—my mother working harder than anyone should have to do to try and supply me with the basics. Although she loves me, loved me then, she was always anxious. Partly because she was so busy, so tired, and partly because she was always looking out for traces of my father in me.'

He couldn't believe he'd revealed so much. It was hard to meet her eyes, to see the sympathy there. He'd never spoken of those days before, not even with Lily—especially not with Lily. She'd never tried to understand him, never really wanted to understand him, found the poverty of his childhood picturesque, the reality would have disgusted her. No wonder he'd preferred not to discuss his past with her. Their marriage had been based on his reliability and dependability. Lily was the one who got to be flaky, Jack the lynch-pin who held them together. It was lonely, un-fulfilling, but he had wanted to give the girls everything he had never had—stability, both parents in their lives—and if that meant put-ting his own barely articulated needs away, that was a price he had been, he was, will-ing to pay.

But not only did he feel that he could be honest with Rosy, he wanted to be. 'Just the thought of setting up a tent, the smell of one, it brings it all back. Not just that day, but also the helplessness of poverty.'

He could see her pause, search for the right thing to say. 'Look, tell me to butt out if you want and I promise not to be offended, but I do get where the girls are coming from. I can't pretend to understand your life. Money was never an issue in my childhood, the op-posite in fact, my life has been pretty luxu-rious. Materially, I had more than I needed or wanted. But, on the other hand, my par-ents were distant, not really ones for cuddles and displays of affection. I went on plenty of holidays, mostly to exclusive villas where I had no one to play with and nothing to do. I didn't want the pool or the luxury, I wanted companionship and fun. I wanted my parents to want to spend time with me. Which is why this cottage was so special, my summers here so important. I had freedom and companionship and adventure and that meant more to me than a private jet and the fanciest hotel suite.'

'My girls get both. The luxury holidays and my attention.' He wasn't over-compensating for his lack of time with money, was he? No, he made time for them, he always had.

'I know they do. But they're still of an age where camping seems like an adventure not a budget option. So why not banish some of those demons and take the girls camping? It might be cathartic. Besides, things have moved on since you were a child.' She reached over for her tablet and opened it, typing quickly. 'What about glamping? All you need to do is turn up and everything is ready, you even get to sleep on a proper bed. Why not surprise the girls?' She passed the tablet to him. 'Look, this place is just a few miles away and you can choose between shepherd huts, yurts, bell tents and even treehouses.'

Jack took a moment to scan the website. Rosy was right, the campsite was a million miles away from the field of his youth, with promises of home-cooked meals delivered to your fully furnished accommodation, underfloor heating in the showers and private baths—to say nothing of the luxury interiors showcased. 'You might be right. Look, there's some last-minute availability this weekend. Why don't you come along too?'

The words hung in the air as Rosy stared at him motionless, her pupils dilated. Part of Jack wanted to recall the words. Hadn't he told himself to keep his distance from her? The girls were clearly getting attached and she would be gone soon. But on the other hand...

On the other hand, he liked her, and it had been so long since he had opened up to anyone the way he had opened up to her. And she liked him, he knew it with every nerve and sinew. He knew by the way her skin flushed the colour of her name when their eyes met, by the way her breathing quickened when he was near, by the way she said his name. Maybe it was foolhardy to invite her along, but he wanted her there—and he so seldom wanted anything other than to keep his girls safe.

And who was to say that if something flared up between them that it could go nowhere? There were still several weeks of summer left. This attraction might peter out as suddenly as it had appeared, and if not? Well, Asturia wasn't that far away. If things progressed maybe they could find a way to work things out.

He grinned, deliberately lightening the atmosphere. 'Honestly, even the thought of luxury camping makes me a little nervous. It would be good to have another adult along who actually wanted to be there.'

Rosy looked down at her beer and then back up. 'I'd love to,' she said eventually, her voice bright and impersonal. 'And shall we invite Sally and her daughter along? As you know, Alice and Clover get along really well, it might be fun to have a group of us. The real camping experience.'

So she didn't want to be alone with him. Maybe he'd misread the signals, or maybe a widower with two daughters was too complicated a package for her. Either way, it was fine.

'Why not,' he said, getting to his feet and picking up the two mugs. 'I'd better deliver these before they get cold.'

She opened her mouth then closed it again. 'Yes, good idea. I promised to show them how to light a fire.'

The intimacy sparked by his confidences

was gone as if it had never been and that was probably a good thing. It was certainly safer. His life was complicated enough without adding in a long-distance relationship or the fallout of a failed short-term fling.

But as he followed Rosy out to the patio where the girls awaited them, a pile of logs at their feet, Jack couldn't help wishing that this connection between them was exactly what it felt like, the start of something, and not just a glimpse of what might have been. The kind of partnership he had never dared dream of.

# CHAPTER FIVE

JACK WASN'T EXACTLY converted to camping but even he had to admit glamping was on another level.

Usually Jack enjoyed the outdoors, cooking on fires, physical exercise, the challenge of making or putting things together. It was just something about the smell of wet tents, bedrolls and sleeping bags that took him back to those nights in their small, cheap plastic tent, shifting uncomfortably on his too-thin mat, pretending to be asleep as his mother cried after a day of trying to make the best of another soggy day. For many years he'd thrown himself into every moment, pretending enthusiasm, not wanting to give her any other reason to cry until along with adolescence came the all-consuming selfishness that often accompanied that stage of life and he'd switched from pretending too much to not pretending enough.

But his girls had none of his reservations and they were more than delighted with the luxury outdoor accommodation. The spacious round bell tents they'd booked were already set up when they arrived, furnished with actual beds, the canvas floors covered with thick luxurious rugs. He'd booked a group pitch with two large tents and one smaller one. The large tents had two bedrooms, both of which easily fitted either a double bed or two large singles, complete with small bedside cabinets and a wooden rail for clothes. The front half of the tent was a large semicircle furnished with a velvet sofa, a couple of large beanbags and a low wooden table that could double as dining or coffee table. The smaller tent Rosy would sleep in didn't have a bedroom, her double bed took up one side of the tent, a loveseat and table the other. All three tents were richly decorated in deep reds, golds and oranges.

At the back of the pitch stood a covered wooden platform that held the kitchen area complete with a sink and running hot and cold water, an oven, fridge and kettle and fully stocked cupboards holding crockery,

cutlery and saucepans. Centred in front of
the tents but far enough away to be safe and
to ensure no smoke wafted into the sleeping
areas was a sunken fire pit surrounded by
sofas. Four posts sat at each corner so a cover
could be pulled over to shelter the sitting area
in case of rain.

'This is *not* how I remember camping,'
Sally said as their host gave them a tour.
The girls had run off to explore the adventure playground with Tansy in charge. Jack
was relieved to see that although as usual she
took the responsibility seriously, she seemed
less solemn, her blue eyes sparkling with excitement and a smile lighting up her thin face.
'I've stayed in holiday cottages more spartan
than this.'

'It really is quite something,' Rosy agreed
as she scanned the information folder the host
had left them with. 'The freezer has ready
meals for emergencies, and there's a takeaway menu as well. Ooh, there's also a proper
woodfired pizza oven by the kitchen and they
can supply dough and all the other ingredients. I vote for pizza tonight.'

The atmosphere between the three adults
was comfortable but Jack could sense Rosy
hanging back, leaving Sally and him to talk.

He knew Sally a little, as was natural when they'd grown up in the same village, but as she was a few years younger they'd never socialised before. Watching Rosy step aside to leave them together, he couldn't help but suspect that she might be trying to set the two of them up. He could see why she might think they would hit it off—after all, they were both single parents and lived in the same place, but although he liked what he knew of Sally, he didn't feel a single atom of the attraction he felt for Rosy.

On the other hand, he could do with friends locally. Nor could he discount the fact that not only was Sally close to Clem, she was also part of the theatre campaign. Whatever Rosy's motivations in inviting Sally along, the night away gave him a great opportunity to discuss his plans with her and see if there was any thawing in opposition. She might even be prepared to be the bridge between Jack and the theatre group.

The afternoon passed quickly and before they knew it the girls were clamouring for food. Jack was more than happy to play with the professional-looking pizza oven and after a busy day of exploring the campsite, farm and beach, Rosy, Sally and the girls made far more pizza than they could all eat while Jack experimented with cooking them until he'd perfected his technique. After dinner he built up the fire and they sat around toasting marshmallows and heating up hot chocolate using the pot provided. The adults took turns telling campfire tales, careful to keep them age appropriate whilst providing the right amount of chill for the setting. Jack couldn't remember the last time he'd had such a carefree evening, or the last time he'd laughed so much as Rosy held them all captive with a comic horror story that by turns made them gasp then giggle. She might claim not to be an actress but she knew how to speak, her voice rich and curiously intimate as if she were pitching her words at everyone individually.

By the time dusk fell all three children were drowsy, even Tansy, and the novelty of sleeping in tents meant sending them to bed was surprisingly easy. They all trooped off happily to the bathing hut with Sally to clean up and put on pyjamas. Clover had begged to sleep with Alice and so Jack kissed her before she headed into the other tent, and he settled Tansy into her bed with a torch and a book.

With the children in bed and the fire starting to die down, Jack opened a bottle of wine. After they'd dissected the day, the conversation naturally turned to the theatre and Jack tried to make his pitch as neutrally as he could, not wanting Sally to feel that she was being set up. But to his relief once he—with Rosy chiming in every now and then—explained what he wanted to achieve, understanding dawned in her intelligent green eyes.

'I think,' she said as she refilled their glasses and handed around some chocolates she'd brought with her, 'that there's been a lot of miscommunication and misunderstanding here, Jack. On both sides.'

Jack couldn't help but agree. 'I dashed in all guns blazing,' he said. 'I saw an opportunity and just wanted to get started. I didn't take account of the recent history, the sense of ownership you all feel—and rightly so. No wonder people think I'm working against you, not with you. But believe me, Sally, I am tired of being seen as a lone wolf. I want the theatre to be a partnership between me and the community. I'm doing it for Polhallow, not despite of it.'

She nodded. 'What you've told me sounds really exciting, and I really think the committee will think so too when they hear it properly. Look, why don't you set up a tour? A chance for you to show us around, just as you showed Rosy around, and then we can sit down and look at the details: what a busier, professional theatre means for the local groups who rely on it, the finances, the legalities. Be honest with us and then let's see where we are.'

It was a fair offer, maybe fairer than he had expected, and Jack gratefully accepted.

'It's exciting to hear it all coming together,' Rosy said, smothering a yawn. 'But even so I can feel myself falling asleep. I think I'll turn in, that delicious-looking bed is calling to me.'

Jack tried to push away the vision of Rosy tumbling into bed, dark curls falling around her bare shoulders. So much for respecting her boundaries, he scolded himself. It was one thing to find her attractive, quite another to allow himself to indulge in fantasies. Besides, although she'd been her usual friendly self all day, there had been a touch of reserve in her manner when she was talking to him, a clear hint that she wasn't interested. A hint he needed to heed.

Rosy's decision was echoed by Sally and Jack decided to head in also and after a quick shower in the luxurious shower block with its underfloor heating and spacious tiled cubicles he pulled on a pair of tracksuit bottoms and a T-shirt and returned to his tent. He could see the glow of Tansy's torch signifying she was still reading and, looking at his watch, realised it was far too early for him to sleep. Instead, he took his laptop to the sofa and set about trying to capture all the questions Sally had asked him around the campfire, making sure he was as prepared for the pitch to the community group as possible, but as he tried to work his mind kept drifting. All he could see was Rosy's face lit by the glow of the fire, hear the echo of her infectious laugh as she told stories, her excitement as they toasted marshmallows, the interest she seemed to take in every small detail of the girls' day.

It was a shame he hadn't met her at a different time and a different place. Rosy was the kind of woman any man would want— beautiful, intelligent, warm, interesting. And what did Jack have to offer? Money? She didn't seem short of that. The truth was he had two goals: to raise his daughters and to redeem his family name. Anything and anyone else would have to be prepared to come in third. It was a lot to ask of anyone, especially a woman like Rosy. No, better he put all thoughts of dating aside until the girls settled and he was established, and he had the time and energy any relationship needed.

Besides, he knew very little about Rosy. In fact, he could count what he did know on one hand and have fingers to spare. She came from a small country he'd barely heard of; she was obviously well-connected, the kind of woman whose family had expectations for her, expectations she accepted, although he sensed she wasn't entirely happy; she was beautiful. But there was so much more to her, kindness and integrity were evident in every gesture. She was the kind of woman who saw a problem and stepped in to help, even helping a virtual stranger struggling with fractious children. But that was it. He didn't know her childhood dreams, her favourite colour. He didn't even know if she was in some kind of relationship right now.

He knew he wanted her.

The words blurred in front of his eyes and so he closed his laptop, and picked up his book, only to find he couldn't concentrate on that either. What he needed was some air. The fire was still glowing and so he grabbed his book and headed back out, picking up his wine glass as he went. But as he approached the fire a figure moved. He wasn't the only one who couldn't sleep. There, wrapped in a blanket, staring into the flames was Rosy. He paused, unsure whether to join her or not, when she turned and smiled, and he knew he was lost.

It was inevitable maybe that Jack would appear as if Arrosa's thoughts had conjured him. It had been far harder than she'd anticipated keeping her distance from him all day. It was as if she were connected to him by some invisible cord. She could sense when he glanced over at her, feel his sudden and unexpectedly sweet smile, couldn't look away from him as he worked to build the fire or make pizza or help the girls on the zipwire. She was constantly aware of him, of his wrists, the vee of his throat, the nape of his neck. Her own gaze lingered on all the exposed vulnerable places as if she was learning them by heart.

'I'm sorry,' he said. 'You probably want to be alone…'

He was giving her the perfect get-out clause and she should take it, but she'd been good all day and it had left her aching with frustration and loneliness. 'I don't have a monopoly on the fire. Join me, please.'

He waited just a second as if checking the offer was real and then sat on the sofa next to hers. 'Not sleepy?'

'Turns out not. How about you? Camping better than expected?'

'Do you think I was being foolish?'

She straightened at that and turned to him in surprise. 'Not at all! We all have our trigger points, Jack, our regrets, memories we don't want to relive. We all keep ourselves safe the best way we know how. Putting your daughters first makes you courageous, not foolish.'

'It's not like we're roughing it. Sometimes I worry that I have gone too far the other way from my childhood, that I sling money at my problems and hope they'll disappear.'

Arrosa wasn't sure what to say. Once again Jack was opening up to her, really opening up to her, an experience so far removed from the polite small talk that dominated her life. And she couldn't help but wonder if he would speak so candidly if he knew who she really was.

'Have you ever spoken to your mother about all of this? About your childhood?' Who was she to ask? She would never discuss her inner feelings with her parents, wouldn't know where to start.

'I've apologised.' His grin was tired. 'Several times. More than apologised. I was able to put money in trust for her, so she doesn't have to work if she doesn't want to. But she told me in no uncertain terms that she had no intention of sitting on her hands all day at barely fifty and suggested if I really wanted to help then I would buy her a business. She sent me the details of the beach bar the very next day. It's no vanity project either, it's thriving and she's already expanding.'

Arrosa laughed. 'She sounds kind of formidable.'

'Oh, she is. I don't think she quite trusts the money I give her is either legal or sustainable. If it's not been earned by her own two hands, or in this case my two hands, she doesn't see how it could be real.'

Arrosa had always been taught that discussing money was rude, but curiosity got the better of her. 'What exactly is it that you do? You can't be more than…what? Thirty? That's some meteoric rise from the childhood you described.'

'Meteoric?' He shrugged but she saw him smile and knew he liked the description.

'Maybe, but honestly it's not that exciting a story. I was interested in programming, and because we couldn't afford for me to have the kind of top-of-the-range computer I wanted I learned to build it for myself from odds and ends. Village gossip will tell you that between fifteen and eighteen I was creating chaos, but the reality was I spent a lot of time in the flat honing my tech skills. At sixteen I started building websites for other people and by seventeen I was already making more than my mother.'

'Impressive.' She meant it. 'But in that case why the reputation? It can't just be your name, can it?'

He blew out a long breath. 'Partly the name, partly me and partly the result of poverty. The fact is, Rosy, that when you're a kid and your clothes are shabbier than everyone else's, and you don't always do your homework because your mother works three jobs and doesn't necessarily have time to help you with your spellings then you are pigeonholed—as lazy or rebellious or whatever. It's not right and it's not fair, but that's how it can be. And when you're alone a lot and bored it's easy to find trouble, and I did.'

'You're right,' she said softly. 'It's not fair.'

Things weren't necessarily better in Asturia, which was why she had spearheaded before and after school schemes. It was a drop in the ocean of what needed to be done, but every child provided with a hot breakfast, with a place to do homework was another child given a chance to succeed.

'The year I was fourteen I was already nearing six foot—I looked older and thought I acted it. I got into a bad crowd, the kind made up of rich summer boys. They were all older than me. You can imagine how cool I thought I was, with no idea that they saw me as a convenient scapegoat. They were loud and drunk and annoying all summer and I tagged along, grateful to be included. Then one of them took his father's car out when he wasn't supposed to and when the police got involved they all blamed me. Of course everybody believed the Treloar boy had been out joyriding. Luckily for me, I got a decent solicitor who pointed out quite clearly that it could have been any of us and got the charges dropped, but everyone immediately knew that I was on the same path as my father.'

Her heart ached for the lonely, misunderstood boy he had been—no wonder redeeming his name was so important to him.

'Only you weren't.'

'No. That scare brought me to my senses—I was lucky not to get a spell in juvenile detention, but worse was the disappointment in my mother's eyes. I swore then that I never wanted to make her look like that again. So over the next few years I kept my head down, programming and honing my skills until at eighteen I got an offer from a start-up to join them. The idea was that we would build apps for businesses and people with ideas in return for a share in the app. It was a bit of a gamble. For every ten apps we put our time and energy into, nine we effectively built for free, and they'd sink without a trace. But when an app made it, it really did. And after a couple of years I stopped just making a good living and started to get rich.'

'And that's what you do now?'

'Not any more. A few years back I took some of the money I had made and looked for ways to invest it in other start-ups, not just apps. An angel, they call it—again I provide the money in return for a share in the company. I started off backing a small local chain of Lebanese cafés who wanted to expand, an organic skincare brand, a tech concierge service. It's similar to the apps; there's a risk that many will fail, others may stay small-time, but the ones that succeed really succeed. I have a team now who scout small businesses with potential for me.'

Rosy leaned forward, fascinated by his drive, his tenacity, his integrity. 'And this is why the theatre means so much—you want to invest in the village?'

'And to show the people here who I am now. Make our name respected, not reviled. And to help create something I am invested in, not just give money to others. Show my girls who I am, make them proud.'

'Of course they're proud. And you should be too. You're an amazing father! How many eighteen-year-olds do what you did? You built yourself up from someone who had barely anything to someone who can afford almost anything, but more importantly to being the best father you could be. Your girls are very, very lucky to have you.'

He didn't answer for a long while. 'Money isn't everything. They don't have a mother; I couldn't give them that.'

There was a lot going on here, more than Arrosa could unpack right now. She knew, she sensed with every fibre of her being that Jack rarely, if ever, opened up like this. What was it about them that made confidences between them so easy? And yet she couldn't repay him with any semblance of truth. It wasn't fair. She couldn't allow the imbalance to tip any further.

'I'm sorry.' She stood up, summoning her best social voice, her best social smile. 'You came here for some time alone with your thoughts. I should leave you to them.'

'Don't go.'

The words were so low she thought for a moment she had imagined them, but then Jack spoke again, his voice almost a guttural growl, reaching out to take her hand. 'Don't go.'

His touch shivered through her, every nerve jumping to attention as her whole body responded to the feel of his fingers threaded through hers, her body hollowing out, an insistent sweet ache pulsing low in her stomach, in her breasts. She almost gasped at the sensation, her own fingers folding around his, anchoring her to him as sensation shot through her.

'I...' She had no idea what to say, what to do. She was all desire, all need, and all the reasons she needed to retreat had floated away, leaving her standing there staring at him helplessly, looking for answers. Jack rose to his feet in one graceful movement and looked down at her, tenderness and need stark in his eyes.

This is a bad idea, she tried to remind herself, but she couldn't remember why that mattered. Why anything mattered but the stars overhead, shining on them as if in approval, the glow of the dying fire, the sweet smell of applewood permeating the atmosphere and the fact that Jack Treloar was looking at her as if she were the moon and the stars.

She stared up at him, drinking in the sharply defined lines of his face, the slope of his cheekbones and the curve of his mouth. Her gaze lingered on his mouth, the sensual curl enticing, inviting her, and she stepped closer, as if of its own volition her hand reaching up to trace his cheekbone, the lines of his jaw.

'Jack,' she whispered, unsure whether it was a plea or a protest. His skin was rough under her fingers, his stubble grazing her as she continued her exploration, returning along his jaw and up until she reached his mouth. He was motionless, eyes dark and full of a desire she had never seen before, never evoked before, and it filled her with a power she couldn't resist as he finally, finally tilted her chin and lowered his mouth to hers.

This was no gentle exploratory kiss but a claiming on both sides that shook Arrosa through even as she matched him, moving so close she could feel his every bone and muscle hard against her. She luxuriated in him, in the owning of him as she explored him, her hands running over shoulders and back, neck and chest, touching and teasing and learning. His hands were wrapped in her hair and she welcomed the slight pull as he wound the curls around his fingers. He tasted of wine and salt, smelt of woodsmoke and something uniquely him that she recognised at a molecular level. She wanted no barriers between them, she wanted him naked and in her, fast and hard and sweet and slow and please God could it be now...

And then, as if the heavens had opened and dowsed her in reality, Arrosa stepped back, all the reasons this couldn't, shouldn't, mustn't happen spinning through her.

'I am so sorry, Jack, I can't. I mustn't.' She reached towards him for one weak moment as she whispered, 'I wish I could', before whirling around and running back to her tent.

# CHAPTER SIX

DESPITE THE EXCELLENT mattress and comfortable surroundings, Arrosa didn't manage to get any sleep that night, reliving the kiss over and over in glorious Technicolor until she was both exhausted and frustrated, filled with unsated desire and regret.

*What had she been thinking?*

The truth was she hadn't been thinking. Instead, she'd allowed herself to be swept away. Turned out a starlit sky, firelight and a handsome man were her own personal kryptonite. Thank goodness she had come to her senses before she'd lost even more control. At least it was just a kiss.

But, oh, what a kiss. The kind of kiss she would remember until her dying moment. Just the thought of it sent flames flicking through her.

It didn't help that Jack kissed in a way guaranteed to make a girl's knees quiver. It wasn't just that he had felt, had tasted, so good. No, the problem was the *way* he'd kissed her. As if kissing her was exactly what he should be doing, was born to do. And she, God help her, had kissed him in exactly the same way.

The truth was it wasn't just a kiss. It was the culmination of a promise, a moment they'd been careering towards from the very first second. A moment she should have done her best to head off, not grasping with both hands as if it was her last chance of happiness.

Only maybe it was. After all, just three weeks ago she had practically proposed to someone she had no interest at all in kissing. Had resigned herself to a loveless, lustless future.

And now? Now she didn't know what she wanted, what to do. No, that wasn't true. She wanted to kiss Jack again. But she couldn't, not while he had no idea who or what she was. Not when her heart seemed so firmly on the line.

To her surprise—and her relief—Jack seemed to act completely normally over breakfast and if the shadows under his blue eyes were darker than usual, well, there were lots of explanations for that. Maybe she'd read him wrong, read the situation wrong. Maybe for him the kiss had been nothing more than a passing whim, he'd just been taking advantage of what was undeniably a very romantic situation. But when Sally volunteered to take the now washed and dressed girls down to see the farm animals, the look he gave Arrosa made it clear that a reckoning was due.

'Fancy a walk?' he asked so casually that if she hadn't been so attuned to him, hadn't seen the pulse beating in his throat, hadn't observed his almost preternatural stillness she might not have known the request was more of a command.

'Sure, let me just get my bag.' She took a few minutes in her tent to breathe and compose herself, before pulling on a cardigan and grabbing her bag. Neither spoke as they made their way to the clifftop path which wound steeply down to a wide pebbly cove and started to make their way across the rocky beach.

'I owe you an apology,' Jack said at last, his jaw tight. 'I misread the situation last night. I didn't mean to make you uncomfortable. Please accept my apologies. It won't happen again.'

There it was, a get-out. Arrosa could say yes, he had misread the situation and they could both pretend she hadn't touched him, hadn't explored the austere planes of his face, hadn't pulled him so tight against her she could still feel him imprinted on her.

But she wasn't a liar. 'You didn't misread the situation. I wanted to be there with you, I wanted to kiss you and I wanted you to kiss me. I was all in, Jack. You don't need to apologise.'

'Okay…' Now he looked confused. 'Was it too soon? Were we moving too fast?' His brows drew together. 'Or are you in a relationship?'

Arrosa didn't know what to say. In one way all of the reasons were true. 'Jack…' She had no idea where to go next. Her hands curled into fists as she took a deep breath. She had to be honest. He was a good man, he deserved the truth from her. 'Yes to all those reasons and no at the same time. I'm not seeing anyone romantically, but my life isn't my own, Jack. That's why I'm here in Cornwall. I'm enjoying a few weeks' freedom before I pledge myself to Asturia. I know, I have always known, that my happiness will always have to come second. And so I shouldn't have kissed you. It was selfish of me because I knew I couldn't pursue it any further, but I just wanted something that was mine, just for once.'

His expression grew even more confused. 'Do you mean you're going to become a nun?'

She laughed, although in some ways the analogy fitted. 'No, although many of my ancestors were. Convents were always a good way to deal with wayward daughters and unwanted wives. Look, Jack, my full name is Arrosa Artega…'

She waited but now he just looked blank. Her name obviously meant nothing to him.

'That's a pretty name,' he said carefully, obviously wondering where this was going.

'Thank you. But this is about more than my name. Okay.' She looked out to sea, trying to find the right words. 'What I am about to tell you can go no further, because it doesn't just affect me. It affects Clem as well. And I really want you to know that I didn't mean to mislead you, I certainly didn't mean for things to escalate between us. But they have and that means you deserve the truth. I'm not a diplomat, Jack. I'm a princess. And in a few weeks' time the laws of my country will be changed to enable me to become next in line to the throne and the next monarch.'

There, it was out, and with it a load she hadn't even known she was carrying.

Arrosa cast a quick glance in Jack's direction to try and gauge his reaction. For a moment she could have sworn she saw hurt flit over his face, only to be wiped away as if it never was as his expression became shuttered.

'I must be very slow,' he said, his voice curiously polite. 'Did you just say you're a princess?'

'I didn't mean to deceive you…' she started but he dismissed her apology with a casual wave of his hand.

'Please don't worry about it, Your Highness. Is that the right title? You'll have to forgive me; I'm not used to addressing royalty.' Each word hammered into her, and she flinched.

'Rosy is fine. Look, Jack, like I said, this isn't just my secret. It involves Clem as well and that means I can't tell you everything, but I really want to try and make you understand.'

'Honestly, there's no need. You've been slumming it with the common people, that's absolutely fine. I hope I helped you relax.' His tone was still ultra-polite, deceptively casual, but she could see by the beat of a pulse in his cheek and the tensing of his jaw that polite was the last thing Jack Treloar was feeling right now.

For a minute she toyed with the idea of turning her back on him, heading back to the campsite and gathering her things before returning to the cottage. In a few weeks' time she'd be back in Asturia and would never see him again. Besides, she didn't owe him any explanation.

But then again, that wasn't exactly true. She'd allowed herself to step into his carefully ordered life. She'd offered to look after his girls, suggested this camping trip. She'd entangled herself with him, gained his trust—and that she knew was a rarity for this proud man.

Now he thought she'd betrayed it, betrayed him, and after he'd allowed himself to be vulnerable in front of her. No wonder he was so cold. She deserved it.

They'd reached the end of the beach, only rocks ahead until the point of the headland. The nearest rock was flat and smooth and Arrosa headed to it and sat, staring out at the horizon. Jack halted a few metres away and tried to calm his tumbling thoughts, quell his instinctive anger.

How could he have been such an idiot? How could he once again have fallen for a woman who didn't have any interest in him apart from as a diversion? A momentary dabble in the real world before stepping back into her gilded life.

It hadn't taken him long after their marriage to realise that Lily had been more interested in his reputation than Jack himself. He had been supposed to be a summer rebellion, the local lord of the manor's daughter slumming it with the village bad boy. Her marriage to him, their baby, a continuation of that rebellion. She'd loved him in her own careless way, but she had never really been in love with him, he knew that now, maybe had always known it.

And now he had once again fallen for a woman who came from a different sphere, who had no long-term interest in him. He was a fool.

'Jack,' she said quietly, almost helplessly. 'Please let me explain.'

His first instinct was to refuse, to walk away, but there was something heartbreakingly vulnerable in her straight-backed posture and so instead he nodded curtly. He owed her nothing, but she could have her say.

She clasped her hands together and stared out to sea for a while, visibly searching for the words, before exhaling softly and looking up at him candidly. 'I came to Cornwall every summer as a child. It's a place that means a lot to me. It was a chance to get away from everything life in Asturia entailed. Like I said to you a few days ago, I had a very privileged but very lonely childhood. One which meant I got to stay in palaces and castles all over the world, but one where I was never allowed to be a child. I always had to be perfectly presented and perfectly behaved. Coming to Cornwall, being Rosy, not Arrosa, was the only time I was free just to be me, to even figure out who me *was*.' She blinked and he could have sworn he saw the glint of tears.

'I always knew that as a girl I couldn't inherit the throne and, apart from the innate sexism of the law, that was more than fine with me. As I got older and got to go to boarding school here in England as well as spend summers here, I could see some kind of freedom in my future. Balancing a career and royal duties is a difficult thing to do, as many minor royals have found before me, and I had no idea what that path would be for me, but I was looking forward to university and figuring it all out. It felt like I had all the time in the world. But I was wrong.' She threw him a quick anxious glance but he couldn't respond, couldn't move, frozen into place by the spell of her words.

'I spent the summer here after turning eighteen and it was golden. I don't know if that's because, when I look back, it was the last time I was truly free, or whether it really was. Clem and I were dating these guys in an intense teen kind of way and the four of us spent the summer surfing and sailing and at festivals. But then my father summoned me home and told me that the right thing to do for our family and for the country was to overturn the primogeniture law retrospectively so that I could become Crown Princess.'

He finally spoke. 'So now you're the heir to the throne?'

'Not quite yet, but soon. In Asturia, the monarch has a lot of political power. The people dislike change. I think it's partly because of where we are positioned, our history is full of war and conflict. It's taken eight years to get to the place where the overturning of the primogeniture law can be ratified. Every opposition party has agreed to support it and the country as a whole agreed in a referendum. During the eight years the change has been debated I have had to be completely perfect in appearance and word and deed. And once I become heir I will have to be even more so. It can be overwhelming at times.'

She blew out a breath. 'Clem thought I needed a break and so she persuaded me to stay here while she is in Asturia pretending to be me—and you are one of just a very small number of people who know that. Jack, if this got out not only would it destroy the public's confidence in me but for Clem the exposure would be life-changing. That I can't tell you any more about, it's not my story to tell, but I hope you see how much I trust you in revealing this much.'

'Clem is pretending to be you? Sure, you resemble each other, but you're hardly identical.' But he could feel his anger starting to thaw. She must have felt desperate to have agreed to such a risky scheme.

'That is definitely the flaw in the plan. But I'd kept my diary free this summer to help me prepare for the ratification, so Clem is being driven out every so often dressed up as me, and that's hopefully enough to keep the tabloids at bay. I've been closely followed, you see, ever since I came of age. A leave of absence would be immediately gossiped about, any kind of hint I needed a break so close to the ratification could lead to the kind of speculation I've spent the last eight years trying to avoid. It's risky, maybe too risky, but the thought of spending six weeks here, being Rosy again one last time, was irresistible. Clem had her own reasons for proposing the switch.'

She looked up at him and he could see the need for understanding, the apology in her expression and he knew her reaction was real. Lily had never cared about being understood, had never apologised to him once, no matter what. But Lily had merely been a rich man's daughter—Rosy was a princess. He had made his own money but he would never be able to create the kind of background and privilege she would need in any future partner.

'There you go, Jack. The whole story. You now know more about me than almost any other person in the world except Clem, my father and my bodyguard.'

'Your secrets are safe with me,' he said at last. 'I can promise you that.'

'Thank you. Jack, I hope you see why I had to step away last night. I couldn't allow us to continue if you didn't know who I am. I didn't want to deceive you any further. But...' She paused and her cheeks pinkened. 'I'd like us to still be friends. I have really appreciated getting to know you over the last few weeks.'

Friends? Was that even possible any more after such an incendiary kiss, after the sharing of such confidences? He'd started to fall for her, hard, and now he was grappling with the fact that she had misled him—and that there was definitely no future for them. Men like him might climb up the social ladder so far, but royalty was definitely a step too far.

Plus, he'd always sworn that if and when he started to date, the girls came first. A relationship with no hope of going anywhere failed that test spectacularly.

But, at the same time, he couldn't just walk away. There was a loneliness to Rosy that he had never really appreciated before, a loneliness that called to him.

'I need to think about it.' He saw her face fall although she tried to hide it. 'It's a lot, Rosy. It was already a lot. You started to change things for me and for the girls in ways I hadn't expected or planned for. And although I knew you weren't planning on living here full-time, that there was no future for us, I couldn't help but wonder that if things carried on the way they'd started maybe somehow there might have been. That we could figure it all out. But now? Now there can never be anything beyond this summer. I know it sounds a little crazy, talking about the future after just a few meetings as if I was still a romantic teen. But there's a connection between us. Isn't there?'

'Yes.'

'So I need time to think this all through.'

'I'm sorry, Jack,' she said, her voice breaking slightly.

Jack wanted to hold her, to promise her that it would all be okay, but that wasn't a promise he could make so instead he simply nodded then turned and walked away.

The irony was that in every other way the camping trip was a great success. The girls seemed happier and more settled, while Jack and Sally were now, if not friends exactly, then friendly, Sally willing to set up a meeting with him and the theatre committee.

But it wasn't lost on Jack that Rosy was responsible for that success—after all, she had suggested the trip and invited Sally along. But thinking of her was like touching a sore spot. He felt hollow inside when he thought about her revelations, the knowledge that it was easier and more sensible to move on with his life without involving her any further in it.

Jack did his best to throw himself into work, but for once it didn't hold his attention the way he had always relied upon it to do. It didn't help that the girls were away; Lily's parents were staying at their Polhallow house and had asked to have their granddaughters for a few days. He had a good relationship with his in-laws now; it was a long time since they'd viewed him as the teenage boy who'd seduced away their daughter.

But with the girls away the house felt too big and too empty and although there were plenty of things he could and should be doing he couldn't seem to get going and this morning was no different. He knew he had to have the promised conversation with Rosy. The problem was, he still had no idea what to say.

It was late morning and already hot as he set out on foot, popping into the café Sally's family owned for snacks and coffees before walking up the hill to Clem's clifftop cottage.

There was no answer to his initial knock

on the door, but the windows were wide open and so Jack walked around the house to the back garden, where he paused, his blood rushing at the sight of a bikini-clad Rosy stretched out on a sunbed, eyes half closed and her face upturned to the sun, a book unopened in her hand.

'Are you open to visitors?'

She started and looked up, wary at first, almost scared, and with a pang of conscience he remembered what she'd said about living under scrutiny, always having to be picture perfect. He was pretty sure that description didn't include lounging in nothing but a bikini, although she did look pretty perfect to him. His mouth dried as he took in the long lines of her body; he'd rather take this relaxed Rosy than any prim and proper princess. Not, of course, that either were his to take.

'I've brought lunch,' he said and held out the paper bag.

For a moment she didn't react, just stared at him before sitting up, her full mouth curving into a wide smile. 'Oh, well, if you brought lunch…'

'It's nothing fancy…' He was barely conscious of what he was saying, just using words to try and bridge the chasm that had sprung up between them.

'Even better.' She pushed herself up to her feet with grace and Jack couldn't tear his gaze away from her long, tanned legs, her exposed midriff, the curve of her breasts showcased by the yellow bikini top. He swallowed as the desire that had never quite subsided flared up, hot and urgent. 'I was just trying to get up the energy to fix some lunch. Shall we eat here?' She gestured to the wrought iron table he was standing next to.

'Perfect.' Jack placed the coffee and bags on the table and watched her as she walked over, pulling an oversized striped T-shirt dress on as she did so.

'Hi,' she said softly.

'Hi.' They looked at each other for a charged moment before taking their seats and Jack tore open the bags to reveal the savoury pastries, olives and marinated tomatoes and peppers he'd bought, pushing a coffee towards Rosy.

She sniffed it appreciatively. 'Flat white, no sugar?'

'I've been paying attention.'

'Thanks.' Colour rose in her cheeks as she took a sip.

Jack pushed one of the bags towards her and they ate, making polite conversation about the quality of the food, the girls' plans for the rest of the week, until the bags were empty and Rosy sat back with a satisfied sigh. 'Delicious, thank you.' She looked down at her hands. 'I'm glad you stopped by. I wasn't sure you would.'

'Neither was I,' he said honestly.

She nodded. 'I get it. My situation is a lot.'

But she *didn't* get it and Jack realised how much he wanted her to understand. 'It is, but Rosy, I've been here before.'

'Here?' Her expression was confused.

'An amusing diversion for a rich, entitled girl who fancied slumming it in the real world.' He enunciated every word. 'I have no intention of ever being that gullible again.'

Understanding and hurt flared in her eyes and he saw her swallow. 'That's not who I am, Jack.' She swallowed again and with an almost defensive toss of her head reached over and took his hand, lacing her fingers through his. 'I don't think I'm entitled, and you are more than my equal in every way. I can't tell you what this thing is between us because I don't know, but I promise that's not how I see you at all. I didn't intend any of this to happen. I shouldn't have allowed myself to get so close to the girls, to allow myself to get so close to you.' Her gaze was devastatingly candid. 'Especially once I realised how attracted I was to you.'

'And I am attracted to you, but it isn't that simple. It matters. Who you are matters.'

'Right now, I am just Rosy, enjoying the sun, and I intend to be her for another two weeks.' She let his hand drop, tilting her chin, and despite her words he could see the proud Princess in every line of her.

But he could see the woman he'd got to know and care for too. 'That's the problem. Because I don't know the Princess, but I do know Rosy. And it's Rosy I want.' He hadn't meant to admit that, but the words were out and couldn't be unsaid.

Her eyes were huge, her lips slightly parted. 'So what do we do?'

'I don't know,' he admitted, 'The sensible thing would have been not to come here at all.'

Rosy sat and looked at him for a long moment. 'Why do you think I see you as a diversion, Jack? You must know how much you have to offer any woman, even a princess. You're rich and good-looking, successful, a great father, fun to be with. Any woman would be lucky to have you.'

'I shouldn't have said that,' he admitted. 'Seeing Lily's parents today brought the past crashing back; it always does, although they mean well.'

'That's understandable. You were married for a long time.'

'You think we got a happy ever after?'

'I know it ended tragically, but raising two wonderful girls together was an achievement.'

It was one way to look at his marriage. He'd always thought of it as an endurance, not an achievement. 'Lily was complicated, which meant our marriage was complicated.'

'How so?'

How could he describe Lily? 'She was wild and beautiful and talented and capricious. She could make you feel like no one else existed or freeze you out completely and you would never know which way it would be.'

'That sounds exhausting.'

'It was.' It was only now that he could look back and see how much his marriage had drained him.

'How did you meet?'

'At the Harbour pub. We set eyes on each other and it was instant fireworks, the way it can only be when you're young and naïve and think *Romeo and Juliet* is a romance not a cautionary tale. Taking up with me was the ultimate two fingers up at her parents and their expectations for her. Her parents wanted her to join the family law firm after Oxford, she wanted to study art. I was her ultimate rebellion, son of the village petty criminal with a reputation of my own. The irony is, she was a lot wilder than me. I think actually I disappointed her in many ways.' He inhaled, thinking back to the naïve young man he'd once been, who thought that love was enough.

'We didn't intend to get pregnant, and she certainly didn't intend to marry me. I was meant to be her summer fun.' He saw Rosy wince and realised she now understood parallels he'd noticed between her situation and his past. 'I think when people gossip about back then, they imagine me whisking her off to some bedsit on the outer edges of London. Instead, I was on such a good salary that we could move to a nice area and once Tansy was born Lily went to art school, just like she wanted. She was talented, but when she left college she was more interested in partying than working and I was making more than enough for her to indulge herself. It wasn't that she didn't love the girls, she just didn't know how to be a mother and didn't care to learn; the children would be brought out at parties and then sent away with the nanny. Just as her childhood had been.'

He reached out and swigged his now cold coffee, grateful for the caffeine. 'Poor Lily, rather than scandalise her parents, in the end they were actually proud of me. Instead of a husband as wild as her, she found herself married to a man with a ridiculous work ethic who made more money than her parents could ever dream of and gave her the kind of life they wanted for her.'

'Were you ever happy?'

It was a long time since he had thought of happiness where his marriage was concerned.

'Sometimes,' he said slowly. 'At least we tried to be.' After all, he'd known her as he knew himself, understood the insecurities that led to her destructive behaviour. 'She loved the girls but motherhood bored her, so I compensated. I went to every play and dance recital, created every holiday tradition. I wanted them to have a perfect childhood. Sometimes I think that somewhere between being the best father I could and my work drive I forgot to be a husband. I didn't want

Lily to feel she'd made a mistake marrying me, I didn't want her to feel trapped, the way my mother did. So I never challenged her about her behaviour, never questioned her about her drinking or the drugs I was pretty sure she was taking on a night out. She took lovers and I pretended not to know. Maybe if I'd intervened she wouldn't have ended up overdosing in a hotel room at the age of twenty-eight.'

Jack couldn't believe the words that had just tumbled out of his mouth, words he had barely dared to think before, let alone say. Words that were his truth. His shame.

But there was no condemnation on Rosy's face. No horror. 'I am so, so sorry, Jack.'

He shrugged, suddenly tired. 'It's been over two years now. Clover barely remembers her. At first, I didn't want to make any big moves, all the books say to give it a year, not to make any sudden decisions in the first wave of grief. And the girls needed their routine. But we lived in a wealthy area, and I could see how young it started. The drinking, the drugs, the dangerous and entitled behaviour. I'm not saying Cornwall doesn't have its problems, I know it does, and I know every school has its own issues. But I wanted to show them a different way before it was too late.'

Rosy reached out and took his hand again and he was glad of the warmth, the firmness of her grip. 'You are not just a good father, Jack Treloar, you are an amazing one. And I am sure Lily would be glad her girls have you looking out for them.'

'You think so?'

'I know so.'

And for the first time in a long time Jack knew so too, freed from the guilt and grief that had plagued him since Lily's death. He was doing his best and that was enough.

# CHAPTER SEVEN

ARROSA SAT STILL for a moment, absorbing everything Jack had told her. Every instinct she possessed told her that she now knew more about Jack Treloar than any other person alive. He'd gifted her his regrets and his hopes and his dreams. It was a precious, fragile gift and she knew how rare it was. Would he have entrusted her with so much if she were staying here? Was the intensity between them fast-tracked by the finite nature of their relationship, that knowledge the clock was ticking, and she was already over halfway through her time here?

And in return Jack knew most of her secrets, apart from Clem's identity. This was as intimate as she was ever likely to be with another human being. And that wasn't something she could just walk away from.

But what else could she do?

'How long are the girls with their grand-parents?'

Surprise—and intrigue—flitted across his expression.

'Until Sunday at the earliest, possibly early next week, depending on how long their grandparents can cope. Losing Lily took a toll on them both, so I like to keep arrangements flexible in case the girls need to come back early.'

'And it's Thursday lunchtime now.' She glanced at her watch. 'If you include this afternoon then you have three days until the end of the weekend.'

Jack raised his eyebrows in bemused query. 'Three days to what?'

'To take a leaf out of my book and get away from it all,' she said. 'Responsibility and duty and shouldering everything yourself is all very well, but if you don't put down your burdens occasionally then you run the risk of breaking.'

'My girls are not a burden.' But, to her relief, he didn't sound angry.

Emboldened, she went on. 'No, of course not. But I don't know a single parent who isn't glad of a break every now and then. We all need to refill the well, Jack. And if your plans for the next few days are just work, work, work how are you going to do any refilling?'

'You think I'm in danger of running dry?' Now he sounded amused as well as curious.

'All I'm saying is that I do know a lot about burnout. I had no idea how close I was myself until the morning I woke up here. It was almost overwhelming, I almost left it too late. But I know now never to let myself get to that stage again.' Arrosa picked up her coffee and drained it. 'You know, I always thought my mother was selfish, disappearing off on retreat every summer without me and without my father. It always seemed an affectation to me, but I understand her better now. For forty-eight weeks of the year she's the perfect Queen. She puts all her own hopes and desires to one side and concentrates on supporting my father, supporting me, making small talk, being the consummate hostess. No wonder she needs four weeks a year when she's just herself.'

Truth was, Arrosa was a little ashamed of how judgemental she'd been. She, of all people, knew that her parents' marriage was no fairy tale but rather a sometimes brutal business arrangement, one broken before it had had a chance to flourish after Zorien had confessed about his love affair with Clem's mother. How could she judge her mother for taking one month a year for herself? She made a quick resolve to call her. They didn't have the sort of relationship which included cosy chats or calls to just check in, but maybe that was something that could change. She might have lost her second mother, but her own mother was still alive and well and Arrosa should not take that for granted.

'So, you think I need a break?'

'Tell me you're not tempted.'

'And you will come with me on this break.'

It was not a question. Which was a good thing because she didn't have an answer.

'That's not…'

But he didn't let her finish. 'Where do you want to go?'

'Jack, it was a suggestion, not a proposition.' But she couldn't deny she was tempted. Very tempted. She'd never been on a mini-break before. And just a few days ago she had resigned herself to not seeing Jack again and now he was offering her the opportunity to spend some real time with him.

She was inexperienced romantically, but she wasn't a fool. She knew what would happen if she agreed.

Her pulse sped up at the thought.

'And it was a good suggestion. I could do with a break, you're right. But I spend a lot of time alone without adult company. If I was going to unwind, really unwind, I might need some help.' His gaze was burning into her. 'So, any requests?'

Arrosa took a deep breath, her chest tight with anticipation. Three days away with Jack—three days and three nights. Without the girls there would be no need to worry about mixed signals and raising expectations. They were both adults and they both knew the score. Had acknowledged how they felt, knew the barriers, that there was no future for them.

Maybe it needed to happen. Maybe if she left Cornwall with this connection still simmering between them, this desire unconsummated, then she would be condemning herself to a constant *what might have been*, a refrain that might run throughout her life. And who knew? Maybe they would burn out as quickly as they'd started.

'Anywhere,' she said and saw Jack relax just a little at the tacit agreement. 'Not abroad as I can't use my passport. If I did the press would instantly be alerted.'

'How did you get here?'

'Private jet and airfield. It's an option but it would take too long to arrange.' Besides, she didn't want to involve the Court or her bodyguard, not in something as private as this.

'UK then. Probably not too far if we only have a couple of days. Besides…'

'Besides, you don't want to be too far from the girls.' She quite understood.

Anticipation buzzed through her. This was nothing Arrosa had experienced before, discussing weekend plans with a man she burned for. 'Let's just get one thing straight,' she told him. 'I know you're a man with refined tastes, but I'm a woman who is very easily impressed. Fish and chips and a decent beach are all I require. Maybe a pint in a really good pub.'

His mouth quirked into a devastating grin and the anticipation intensified. 'You don't need your own concierge service?' She shook her head. 'Chauffeured limo? Michelin stars? Personal spa?'

'None of the above. If you could manage a clear sky and some stars I'd be very grateful, and I prefer my bed to be freshly made, but otherwise anything goes.'

His gaze softened into something so tender it hurt. 'Leave it with me.'

Jack disappeared to make arrangements and Arrosa quickly tidied away the lunch things, texting Sally to see if she'd be able to feed Gus for just a couple of nights, and went upstairs to pack, singing to herself as she did, her feelings so intense she could barely concentrate. Thank goodness she could use Clem's wardrobe; her own array of tiny beach dresses, shorts and bikinis clearly wouldn't take her very far.

Clem favoured vintage cuts, bright colours, whereas Arrosa usually dressed in more subtle tones and cuts, but then again, she'd never really had a chance to figure out her own taste. Once the project to turn her into the perfect Crown Princess had commenced, a stylist had been employed to make sure that Arrosa trod the fine line between fashion and appropriateness and so although her clothes were made just for her, and although she was always completely up to the minute in terms of cut and colour, there was something depressingly interchangeable about the dresses and little jackets, tailored trousers and neat jumpers she usually wore. Looking through Clem's eclectic mix of dresses and skirts, silky little tops and jumpers was a lot of fun and, before she knew it, she had selected enough for a week away, let alone just a couple of days. But, then again, she had no idea where they were going.

Jack collected her an hour later, refusing to give her any hints, although he drove deeper into Cornwall and not away from the county until they finally reached Penzance. He continued winding his way through the town, pulling in at a car park near the docks.

'We have to leave the car here,' he said as he swung their cases out of the boot. 'They don't allow visitors' cars where we're going.'

Arrosa looked towards the dock and the ferry sign, excitement mounting. 'The Isles of Scilly? Oh, Jack! That's perfect. Clem and Simone went one spring, and their photos were amazing!'

She'd always wanted to visit the small cluster of islands at the southern tip of Britain. Famous for their microclimate and wildlife, something about the islands had always appealed to her.

'It turns out that finding something last minute for a weekend in early July isn't that easy, but luckily I know people who know people. Sure this is okay?'

'It couldn't be more okay,' she said as he took both cases and headed towards the boarding gate for the ferry.

It was a windy couple of hours on a surprisingly rough ocean, but Arrosa drank in every second, laughing as her hair escaped the coil she'd fastened it into and whipped around her face. She, Arrosa Artega, was heading off on a romantic weekend with a man she had started to care for and right now everything was perfect.

Rosy's enthusiasm was infectious. She loved everything, from the ferry journey over to St Mary's and the transfer to the smaller boat which took them to Tresco, exclaiming at the seals and dolphins they spotted in the waves. She didn't even mind the mile-long walk to the cottage Jack had managed to borrow, despite the stiff climb and her bulky case, waving away his offer of help.

'Don't treat me like a princess,' she told him.

'It's chivalry,' he protested.

'I'm quite capable, and I'm the one who overpacked.'

Finally, they reached the whitewashed cottage which sat alone on the headland. It had been cleaned and prepared for them and Jack retrieved the key from the keysafe, opening the door and standing back, allowing Rosy to precede him.

He followed her into the small but perfectly formed cottage. The ground floor was one room, kitchen, dining space and lounge combined, with floor-to-ceiling windows framing the dramatic ocean views on one end and the cliffs on either side. It was comfortably yet stylishly decorated and Rosy turned to Jack, eyes glowing.

'I love it. I can't wait to explore!'

You would never think that Rosy was a princess, used to the best of everything, Jack reflected as she exclaimed in delight, exploring every inch of the cottage, dashing from view to view, opening cupboards, examining the bookcases.

'It's not too small?'

She shook her head, her delighted smile widening even further if that was possible. 'You know, even though I moved out of the château when I was twenty-one, I still have four bedrooms in a house where no one comes to stay, and a couple of downstairs rooms I don't even use. I don't need or want a big house; cosy suits me fine.'

And that was part of what he liked about her. She wasn't influenced by how much something cost, but by what it meant.

'That's good to hear because this place is certainly bijou,' he said. 'And of course,' he added hurriedly, not wanting there to be any misunderstandings between them, 'I'll take the pull-out bed.'

There was only one bedroom, taking up the whole of the upper floor, with a luxury shower room off it—the bath was on a raised platform by the window in the bedroom so the occupant could fill it with water and the decadent-smelling bath oil and lounge comfortably, looking out to sea.

'The pull-out?'

He nodded towards the sofa. 'It turns into a bed.'

She held his gaze levelly, but he could see a trace of uncertainty in her eyes. Not, he thought, uncertainty about what she was about to say, but more uncertainty about his reaction.

'It's a big bed,' she said deliberately. 'I would say it's big enough to share.'

Jack swallowed at the hope in her gaze. It wasn't an unexpected offer. After all, this was no platonic getaway. The prospect of consummating their connection had been there since the moment he'd suggested she join him for a getaway, the moment she'd accepted. Staying in a small, isolated cottage in the middle of nowhere, a cottage made for lovers, just set those expectations more firmly. But it was the first time either of them had alluded to it out loud.

'Okay.'

Her smile was mischievous. 'I mean, you can sleep on the sofa bed if you prefer.'

'I'm sure the bed will be fine.'

Her dimples flashed. 'Good, I'm glad that's settled.'

Jack continued to watch her as she whirled around the cottage, still discovering new things to exclaim at in surprise or approval. He needed to concentrate on the here and now and deliberately, very deliberately, not think about what he was doing. Not think about the promise that hovered over them, the evening just a very few short hours away.

This trip was impulsive, frivolous, dedicated to momentary pleasure, all things Jack rarely allowed. He liked his life planned and organised and deliberate, had done ever since the day the policeman had told his fourteen-year-old self that he could be facing a lengthy spell in youth detention. The next two hours, alone in a cell waiting for his mother, afraid of the sadness and, worse, the resignation he knew he'd see on her too-worn face had changed him. He'd realised what an impulsive fool he had been, played with by older, richer boys who saw him as little more than amusement and had no compunction in using him as their scapegoat. He'd seen his future stretched out before him, full of rooms like that, spells in and out of jail, like his father had before him, leaving a trail of broken hearts and broken potential behind him. He'd vowed then and there that that would not be his destiny and everything he'd done since had been a rebuttal of the policeman's words.

The only time he'd allowed himself to step off the path he'd set himself was when he'd met Lily. That summer his future had seemed assured, his job lined up and already enough money saved to change his life. But even that hadn't derailed him. When he'd found out Lily was pregnant he'd just adjusted his plans, used the prospect of becoming a father to motivate him even more.

Now he was stepping off the path again for a very different woman. A woman who was considered and responsible, one who accepted her responsibilities and fate, who wasn't trying to outrun her destiny but to meet it with grace and acceptance.

'You look very pensive.' Rosy came to stand next to him, close but not touching. For two people away on a romantic weekend they were very careful not to touch, but he could feel the air around them tense.

'I'm just thinking what a lucky man I am,' he said, and her face softened.

'Don't you forget it.'

'It's a little late to explore the island,' Jack said. "But we have this place until Sunday, so shall we head out and get some food? There are a couple of really good restaurants; they are probably fully booked but I'm sure I could pull some strings.'

'You know, I don't want a fancy restaurant.' Rosy put a hand on his shoulder and looked up at him almost shyly. 'I wasn't kidding earlier. What I really, really want is fish and chips, maybe a beer, sitting on the beach, watching the boats go by. Does that sound really boring?'

'No,' he said slowly. 'That sounds perfect.'

Too perfect. This was a summer idyll, nothing more, but with every passing moment he knew he was falling harder for her.

* * *

'They were the best fish and chips I ever had in my entire life,' Rosy said, leaning against him with a contented sigh, and Jack agreed. The takeaway had been perfectly cooked, slightly crispy chips melting in the middle and covered with the perfect amount of salt and vinegar, delicately flaked fish in melt-in-the-mouth batter accompanied by a tart locally brewed beer with just the right amount of hops. Add in the soft sandy beach, the stunning sunset and the sea views and Jack realised he'd never enjoyed a meal more. Nor had he ever felt anything like the anticipation for what came next. Much as he wanted to drag her back to the cottage and kiss her until neither of them could speak, he also wanted to enjoy the wait a little longer.

'Fancy trying the local pub?' he asked and she agreed, exclaiming how lucky they were to find a small table by the window as he fetched the drinks, like any normal couple out on a date, making small talk about books and films and dreams.

'Have you ever thought about who you would be if you weren't you?' Jack asked after a while and Arrosa stared at him in confusion.

'If I wasn't me?'

'I'm trying to be discreet,' he said. 'You know, if you didn't have to do the job you have to do.'

'Oh.' Her face fell a little. 'It's not something I think about,' she said at last. 'It is what it is, and I can't change it so I try not to waste time wishing for something else. But I'm glad I don't have one overwhelming passion. If Clem was me, for instance, and couldn't act, then it would have destroyed her. I wasn't overjoyed about the closing down of other paths, but I accepted it. I think if I can keep some semblance of normality in my life, like living in my villa, that kind of thing, then I'll be okay.'

'That's a very healthy attitude.'

She shrugged. 'I could have said no to my dad, I guess, but then how could I advocate for change if I didn't want to be that change? I can't run away from who I am, from my responsibilities, at least not for ever. How about you? Any unlived dreams?'

'Obviously, I was married and a father young, so like you, I suppose, I accepted responsibility then and learned not to waste time on daydreams. But the truth is my girls give my life meaning and purpose. I wouldn't want to imagine a world where they aren't my life. I guess,' he said slowly, 'what we have in common is that even if circumstances don't work out the way we thought they might, we know how to make the best of the situation we're in. That's pretty rare in my experience.'

Rosy held up her drink. 'To the cards we're dealt'.

He clinked his glass against hers but as they made the toast couldn't help wondering if they would be so philosophical when Rosy left for good.

Her gaze was fixed on his as she finished her drink. 'You know I don't want another drink here. Let's get back.'

'You sure?' he asked, and they both knew he was asking about more than the drink.

'Yes,' she said. 'I have never been surer. Let's go.'

# CHAPTER EIGHT

NEITHER SPOKE AS they walked back in the rapidly darkening dusk, anticipation colouring every step, every movement, every glance. Arrosa was attuned to Jack's every move, breath and glance. Desire swirled, hot and intense, throughout her entire body, pooling in the pit of her stomach, causing flickers of heat in every nerve, her breasts heavy and almost painful. It was like some specific kind of torture, almost painful, apprehension mingling with anticipation.

They still hadn't spoken by the time they reached the cottage and Jack once again unlocked the door and ushered her in. Arrosa swallowed nervously as she slipped off her wrap and stood slightly awkwardly in the middle of the lounge watching Jack as he closed the door behind him and moved towards her, graceful, masculine and seemingly unaffected by the nerves that now consumed her.

He reached her and paused, tilting her chin up so that he could look in her eyes. It took everything Arrosa had to meet his dark gaze.

'We don't have to do anything you don't want to,' he told her, and she loved him for it.

'But I do want to,' she said and before she could change her mind wound her arms around his neck, bringing him closer, until once again she was kissing him the way she had wanted to since their first kiss a few days before.

Just like the kiss at the fire, there was no gentle introduction as once again the kiss ratcheted from nought to sixty without passing go. His mouth was strong and possessive, his hands sure and knowing, and even though he was only touching her back and waist, her whole body ached for more, arching towards him. She found herself tugging at his shirt, impatient to get to the skin underneath, to run her hands over the smooth muscled planes of his body, needing to know him in every way, to discover every inch, to make him hers. She dragged her mouth from his, pressing kisses along his jawline as she finally wrenched his shirt off, leaving her free to explore the skin underneath.

He hissed as her hands moved lower, now pulling at his belt. 'Rosy, we have all the time in the world.'

But they didn't! They had here and now and if they were lucky a couple more weeks and that was it. What had she been thinking of, waiting an entire month? They could have been here already; this could be one moment in a long line, not the first. She pressed even closer, holding his face between her hands as she kissed him harder, impatient for him to touch her in all the places that ached for him.

Jack didn't protest any more, kissing her back with equal intensity, finally, finally sliding his hands up her back, his clever fingers tracing every inch of skin until she was boneless with desire and only then sliding down with excruciating slowness to explore every rib before slowly, so slowly, inching back up towards her aching breasts. Arrosa moaned as his finger finally brushed against one tight nipple, arching into him as sensation engulfed her. 'Can we go upstairs?'

She felt his rumble of amusement, 'I feel like I should be sweeping you up and carrying you to the bed,' he said. 'But that spiral staircase isn't made for grand gestures. Ladies first.' She felt cold as she stepped away from him, her legs shaky as she made her way upstairs and turned to face him, all too aware of the giant bed which dominated the room.

For all her bravado, and her desperation to get past the niceties, her nerves had returned in full and her hands shook as she unzipped her dress. Jack stood near the staircase watching her, his expression unfathomable.

'What's wrong?'

'I'm a little nervous.' She tried to smile but his expression darkened.

'Rosy, I meant every word. We don't have to do anything you don't want to do. I have no expectations.'

'I know.' She bit her lip. Now it came to it, she couldn't quite find the words. 'It's just I've not done this before.'

She flushed hot at the surprise in his eyes, followed by understanding. 'I see.'

'It's a princess thing, you see,' she said hurriedly. 'I don't really date. The only people that ask me out are those that see the Princess, not the person, and that is possibly the least sexy thing I could imagine. Plus, there's always that fear in the back of my mind, if things don't work out, what if they go to the press? I couldn't bear any *My night of passion with the Princess* headlines. So there's never been anyone I've been willing to risk it for before. Not before you.'

His eyes darkened even more as he took a

step closer. 'I don't see the Princess. I see the woman. I see you, Rosy. And it's you I want. But if it makes you feel better, I am just as nervous.'

'You are?' It was her turn to be surprised.

'Of course I am. For a start, you are one hell of a woman and that would make any man nervous. Secondly, now I know it's your first time I want to make it as special as I can. And thirdly, in a way it's a first time for me. You see, I've only ever slept with Lily.' Her gaze was glued to his but all she could see was candour and honesty.

'Really?'

'Really.'

'But…'

'It's a little bit like the princess thing, I suppose. When I was younger the kind of girls who were attracted to my reputation weren't the kind of girls I wanted to be with. Then I was married to Lily for ten years and, although it was an imperfect marriage, I took my marriage vows seriously. Since she died the girls come first and I haven't even considered dating. So, it's a first for me as well.'

'Then I'm the one who's honoured.'

It was as if their confidences had broken the ice. Her shyness had gone, her trepidation disappeared; all she wanted was this man now. She laughed a little breathlessly as he backed her onto the bed, luxuriating as she felt his weight upon her, as he kissed her until she could barely think any more, the last layers of clothing expertly discarded until there was nothing between them.

'Is this okay?' Jack kissed his way down her throat, one hand expertly palming her breast, and she moaned.

'Yes.'

'And this?' He drew her nipple into his mouth and she bucked as sensation flooded through her, barely able to articulate assent.

'And this? And this?'

He continued to murmur endearments, checking in as he explored her with a languid ease that left her panting and writhing until she was begging him to just please do it *now*, crying out as he finally entered her, pulling him closer, demanding more.

'Are you sure you haven't done this before,' he said many hours later as they lay tangled together. 'I must be a very good teacher.'

She laughed, raising herself onto one elbow to look down on him and kiss him. 'I didn't say I was a total novice. I'd done stuff.'

'Stuff? What stuff?'

'Do you want me to show you?'

His smile was pure wolf. 'Yes, please.'

She stayed there for a moment, drinking him in, luxuriating in his evident desire for her, for Rosy, not the Princess, and then bent her head, flicking her tongue along his chest and enjoying his intake of breath.

'As you wish.'

What happened in the Isles of Scilly was supposed to stay in the Isles of Scilly, but although they had both agreed that it would be too difficult to carry on their relationship back in Polhallow, Jack managed to find time nearly every day to sneak over to the cottage to make love to Rosy. Despite their good intentions, one weekend together had not been nearly enough time and they couldn't bring themselves to stop, not with the time till Rosy's departure ticking away faster and faster, the nights and days flying by at unbearable speed.

They were very careful not to let anyone suspect what had happened, was happening, not to show by a single glance or touch that there was anything more between them than friendship. It was hard, fiendishly hard. Jack allowed his gaze to linger on Rosy, sitting at his kitchen table helping Tansy learn her lines for a forthcoming audition. She looked like summer personified in a lemon sundress, her curls escaping from her ponytail, and it was all he could do not to kiss the tempting back of her neck. He'd had his doubts about whether Rosy should see the girls regularly with her departure so close, but he couldn't deny that she had a knack with them, especially Tansy, and as they didn't know that there was more between their father and Rosy it seemed a shame to deny them the friendship.

As Jack had hoped, the sea air and the change of routine was working miracles with his oldest daughter and she was visibly blooming before his eyes. Thanks to her surf lessons and the theatre group, she'd started to make friends and she'd also stopped second-guessing his every decision and was acting more like a sister than a mother to Clover. Their relationship seemed far more normal now for siblings, and he was surprisingly relieved to hear them bicker over everything from which film to watch to what he should make for dinner.

'That's really good, Tansy.' Rosy closed her copy of the script and smiled at his daughter. 'You're going to be a real asset to the theatre group, I can tell.'

Tansy's face lit up. 'You think?'

'I know. Don't forget I grew up with an actress. I see the same determination in you that I saw in her.' She picked up her phone. 'I need to get back. Make sure you let me know how the audition goes. Bye, Jack.'

He raised a nonchalant hand as if he hadn't got plans to spend the evening at hers once he'd dropped Tansy off at her new friend's house, a fellow aspiring actress she'd met at the theatre.

'Dad…' Tansy was watching him '… I like Rosy. I really like her.'

'We all do, she's been a good friend to us.'

'Dad, you know, it's okay if you want to start dating someone. Clover and I wouldn't mind. Not if it was someone like Rosy. You like her, don't you? I mean, *like* her like her.'

Jack stilled. His girls had idolised their elusive, fragile mother. 'Tansy…'

'Mummy's been gone for a long time now. I just wanted you to know we'd be okay if you wanted to see someone.' Her blue eyes were filled with hope and Jack's chest tightened. This was everything he'd tried to avoid.

'Rosy is great, and you're right.' He made the decision not to lie to his daughter. 'I do like her, and if things were different, who knows? But her life isn't here, kiddo. She doesn't belong in Polhallow, she has a really important job in Asturia. So, friends is all we can be and that's great. You can never have too many friends.'

'But you don't have to stay here. Couldn't you do your job in Asturia?'

'Honey, we've only just moved here. We don't want to keep moving.'

Tansy shrugged. 'I'm just saying that if you and Rosy did like each other we could move again.'

Jack searched for the right words, not wanting to quash her honesty nor raise her hopes. 'Thank you for saying that, but we have only known Rosy a few weeks. It would be far too early, even if we *were* dating, to be talking about moving. Sometimes, Tansy, the timing just isn't right, and you just have to accept that. It's part of life. What time are you due at Clara's?'

But she clearly wasn't going to drop the topic. 'Clover thinks you should get married, but that's because she wants to be a bridesmaid. It's too early to think of *that*, but I think it's silly not to at least try if you like each other. Rosy likes being with us. She looked all worried when we first met her and now she laughs all the time. I like it when we all laugh. It's fun to be in a big group.'

Guilt pierced him. He'd done his best to provide his daughters with everything they needed. More, a good education, the kind of exclusive experiences most children dreamt of. And the three of them were a tight bubble of love and laughter. But outside of that bubble there wasn't a great deal of humour or socialising. Lily had preferred the dramatic to the everyday and was so often absent, and there was no extended family of cousins and uncles and aunts. Nor did they have a large social circle. In some ways, their childhood was as solitary as his had been. As Rosy's had been.

'Tansy, I'm glad you and Clover like Rosy so much.' He searched for the right words. 'And it's good to know that you'd be okay if I started dating again. It's not a priority, but who knows what will happen? But darling, it can't be Rosy. She goes home next week.' He hated to disappoint her, but he also needed to nip this in the bud. Any prevarication and they might carry on hoping.

'Like I said, her home is far from here and we are building lives here. Friendship is just as important as romance, Tansy. Don't forget that. Romances can flare and disappear as if they never were, but a good friendship lasts for ever.'

Tansy's eyes were clouded with disappointment as she nodded and ran upstairs to pack a bag for the night ahead. Jack watched her go, heart heavy. He'd done this, roused hopes in his girls he couldn't fulfil. They'd tried hard to be discreet but the connection between them was so palpable even his girls had picked up on it.

There were just a few days left. They needed to be more discreet than ever. And he needed to heed the words he'd said to Tansy because they were true. He and Rosy might not be able to have a real romance but maybe they could be friends. Hell, he had few enough of them. Maybe there would be a way of keeping her in his life, because there was no way he was ready to let her go for good.

# CHAPTER NINE

IT WAS ANOTHER beautiful afternoon. In fact, every afternoon over the last week had been beautiful. There had been something restorative about the light summer rain that had punctuated the week before, something dramatic about the sheets of rain that had cleaned the beaches and outside tables the day before that. Every type of weather seemed fresh and restorative. But today was the best afternoon of all: hot but not humid, sunny but gently, glowing not glaring. And every atom in and around Arrosa was glad to be alive.

She laughed a little self-mockingly as she shook flour into the mixing bowl and reached for the cubed butter she'd cooled earlier. She knew she was being slightly ridiculous—more than slightly—but she couldn't help it. And if this was what good sex, lots and lots of sex, did to a person then she'd clearly been

missing out all those years. Those long after-
noons of listening to speeches, soothing the
overinflated egos of local bureaucrats and top
politicians, of dress fittings and hair appointments and ribbon-cutting would have been
a lot easier with this sated languor playing
through her body. The radio switched to another song, one she loved, and she joined in,
singing loudly as she continued to rub the
butter into the flour.

Jack was coming over later, and she wanted
to wow him with home-made scones as if
they were a real couple, as if this was just
another date, not the beginning of the end.
Because the truth she was denying was that
Arrosa was running out of time. Next week
Clem would return and they would switch
back, and she would have to say goodbye to
her life here, to her friends—and to the small
family who had captured her heart. How had
this happened? What had started out as a flir-
tation had developed too quickly and too intensely. She knew Jack felt it too—the other
evening he had suggested that maybe there
was a way they could remain friends once
she returned.

In one way she wanted to, but in another
she thought it would be harder to have Jack

in her life but not by her side. She spent long hours imagining introducing Jack to her life in Asturia, the girls to her pretty lakeside villa. Her imagination worked when they were in the palace grounds; it was the wider world where it failed completely. Her life was one of formality and discipline; there was little fun there for two girls still learning how to smile again after tragedy had robbed them of so much.

Any consort of hers would spend their life in the spotlight. Every word, every look and expression dissected. Jack was an intensely private man; how could she ask him to give up that privacy and allow his past to be raked over after just a couple of weeks of an idyllic summer romance? She couldn't.

So she needed to push any daydreams of the future aside to enjoy the here and now. To focus on the good part, to remember that Jack had shown her that she was capable of loving and being loved. That there was a living, breathing woman in the proper Princess.

Arrosa's hands stilled. Where had that thought come from? Capable of *love*? Attraction, of course. Desire? Liking? Yes and yes. She really, really liked him and she really, really desired him. But she couldn't have fallen in *love*, not in just five weeks.

But, then again, how could she *not* have fallen in love with Jack? Her mind ran through memories like a movie montage: Jack strolling over the beach, Clover on his shoulders, explaining the tides. Jack handing over his ice cream to Clover because she'd dropped the one she'd bought. Jack hearing Tansy's lines yet again. Jack spending many anxious moments deliberating over whether the hoodie he was buying her was too babyish or too adult or just right. Jack pacing on the stage, explaining his vision, lit up with an enthusiasm that inspired her too. Jack sitting opposite her, confiding things she instinctively knew he had never confided to anyone before. Jack holding her, touching her, kissing her, making her feel like a woman reborn.

How could she *not* love him? It was impossible. As impossible as loving him.

With a herculean effort she pushed the thought away, resuming singing and rubbing the sticky mixture, focusing fiercely on the here and now until the sound of her phone made her look up and she realised she'd missed a call. She used her voice to activate the voicemail, still humming along to the music.

'Arrosa?' And, just like that, her mood evaporated.

'Papa,' she breathed as she began to brush the mixture off her fingers. Even though he couldn't see or hear her, it was as if she could sense his disapproval down the line.

'I hope you've had a good break, Arrosa. I wish you'd been a little more discreet, but indiscretion seems to run in the family at the moment.'

Shamed heat flared up instantly. Of course he'd had her followed, she'd expected it. And yet she'd also allowed herself to forget it. Had her father's spy followed her to Tresco? Had they watched her sitting with Jack on the beach? Flirting with him in the pub? Had they seen them the day after, wrapped around each other, unable to let go of each other's hands as they explored the island? Reported on the kisses and the way they touched?

Of course they had. The thought filled her with revulsion.

'Well, it doesn't matter now, because I'm going to say to you exactly what I said to your sister. Holiday time is over, Arrosa. It's time to come home.'

Her hands dropped to her sides, still sticky and covered with the flour and butter mixture. 'No,' she said to the phone, as if it weren't a recorded message she was answering. 'It's too early, I've got another week.'

'People are beginning to talk, Arrosa. Your sister's absences from the palace with no explanation are beginning to be noticed. I need you back here doing your normal day-to-day duties to allay those suspicions. And you are allowing your personal life to become public. It just needs one person to recognise you in the background of one photo or video for the whole thing to blow sky-high. You are staying in one of the most photographed spots in the UK, the chances of you being spotted with this man you're spending all your time with are too high.'

She had nothing to say. Of course, as usual, he was right.

'Look...' and suddenly he sounded kind and that was so out of character it felt worse than his usual hectoring tones '...I allowed the charade to go ahead because I understood that you needed a break. But you had your fun, and your sister's had hers, and it's time for you both to go home. Henri will be escorting your sister to Cornwall tonight and will collect you. I'll see you tomorrow.'

The message came to an abrupt end. Mechanically, Arrosa carried on making the scones, but she couldn't have said what ingredients she added. Instead, her mind repeated the inescapable facts. Her time was up. By this evening she would be back in Asturia and that would be it, her life prescribed and small and necessary. She'd known it was coming. She'd thought she was prepared.

Her phone pinged with a couple of follow-up messages from her father, arrangements for meetings over the next few days, but she ignored them, watching the scones turn the perfect shade of brown and pulling them out of the oven. They looked and smelled delicious, but she had no appetite, no sense of achievement.

The desolation overtook her as she sank onto a chair, eyes dry and sore. She wasn't ready to go home, not yet. How could she be? She'd fallen in love and before she'd even had time to come to terms with what that meant she had to walk away.

Her phone rang again and this time after a few seconds' hesitation she picked it up, noting Akil's name on the screen. She summoned up her best princess persona.

'Akil, is everything okay?' She winced at the words. She knew Clem had grown increasingly close to Akil. She was unlikely to be looking forward to coming home either.

His voice was grim. 'Not exactly. Have you spoken to your father?'

'Funny you should ask that. He's left me a voicemail and a couple of messages, telling me it's time to come home.'

'He's told Clem the same thing, that her time here is up.'

'I guess we always knew it wasn't for ever,' Arrosa said, unable to keep the unhappiness from her voice.

'You certainly couldn't keep this pretence up for ever. At some point people will want to see the Princess's face. Clem needs to be able to leave the Palais without disguises and subterfuge. But that doesn't mean that things should have to go back to the way they were. Don't you agree?'

Agree? With what? 'What do you mean?'

'We're about to begin a new era here in Asturia, spearheaded by you, Arrosa. Don't you think it's time for a new start in every way?'

'Is this about Clem?'

'I love her. And I think that she loves me, but she won't stay here with me, she won't put her happiness first, because your father has told her that if anyone finds out who she is the scandal would be too much for you and she loves you too much to be a burden to you.'

Of course he had said that. *Of course* he had. Zorien Artega, the arch manipulator. 'But that's not it at all, Akil. I would love everyone to know who she is, I am so proud of her, but how could I do that to her? Clem has never been the target of the press. She's never been followed anywhere, she's never been commented on, she's never had her outfits dissected, her love life speculated on, her every expression misinterpreted until she had to learn to show no expression at all. She has a freedom that I can never have, and that freedom is the greatest gift I can give her. If anyone knew who she was, she'd lose that.'

'I think that should be her decision, don't you? Arrosa, don't you see, you're protecting her and she's protecting you and the only people losing out are the two of you?'

'And this is all altruistic on your part?'

'I don't deny that I would like her to stay in Asturia, that I would like to carry on seeing her, but this is beyond us, whatever we are.

She is all alone, Arrosa. She is going back to Cornwall with no family, no one who really cares about her apart from you and me.'

Arrosa looked around the cosy cottage filled with memories. Akil was right. Clem's future had stuttered to a halt the day her mother was diagnosed. She had friends, many of them, but her family—and the man who loved her—were hundreds of miles away. 'What do you want me to do?'

'I'm going to go and see your father to tell him that I think he should come out and acknowledge her if that's what she wants. And then I am going to see if I can persuade your stubborn sister to give us a chance. I just need to know: will you back me up or not?'

Arrosa didn't hesitate. 'If that's what Clem wants, then yes. I will.'

'Thank you, that's all I needed.'

Akil rang off and Arrosa sat and stared at her phone, her heart filled with hope and happiness for her sister even as she could see no reciprocal happy-ever-after for herself. After a long time, she pulled her phone to her and typed a message to Clem.

I just want to say that whatever you do decide I have your back, always. I'm proud of you and I'm proud to have you in my life and I am happy to shout it from the rooftops to anyone and everyone if that's what you want. I love you, big sis.

The reply came back quickly.

Right back atcha!

Arrosa smiled and sent another text, this time to Akil.

Whatever Clem wants, whatever Clem decides, I will always back her.

She had no idea what would happen next, but if Clem found happiness then at least one good thing would come out of this swap. That had to be enough.

Something was wrong and Jack couldn't put his finger on what it was. Rosy looked the same as usual, delectable in a flowery maxi dress, her hair down and cascading over her shoulders. She'd set the table with freshly baked scones, fresh fruit, jam and cream, flowers from the garden in a jug in the centre. But even so something was definitely wrong, her smile mechanical and her eyes dull as she kissed him. 'I made you scones.'

'They look delicious,' he said cautiously. 'Can I have one?' But his appetite had gone even as he split it in two, adding cream and jam to the still-warm scone. Rosy had retreated to the sink, washing up, her hair veiling her face. 'Hey, why don't you come sit with me?'

She stayed silent and every quiet second filled him with dread until she finally turned, her face still completely expressionless. 'I have to go home, Jack.'

'I know,' he said, searching for the right words. 'I've always known.' Although he realised, with a shock, he was by no means ready. He'd known this time together was finite, and told himself that was okay, but the truth was, like a child ignoring something unpleasant, he'd not allowed himself to look forward, hoping that maybe they would mutually decide they'd had enough, that this relationship would just peter out.

But he knew that wasn't going to happen, not yet at least. Maybe not ever.

'I have to go home tonight.'

'What? Why?' Had he heard right?

'My father has summoned me. He's sending Clem home and he wants me back.'

'You're a grown woman. You can go when you're ready.'

'It's not that simple. I have responsibilities and a destiny I can't walk away from, no matter how much I may want to.'

'*Do* you want to?'

She didn't answer for a long moment, then her mouth curved into a sad reminiscent smile.

'In the pub in Tresco you asked me who I would be if I could be anybody I wanted. And I told you that I don't waste time on such thoughts, that it's a waste of energy imagining anything different. Remember?'

He nodded.

'I meant it, Jack. That's how I live my life. But over the last couple of weeks I've allowed myself to imagine a different life, imagine what it would be like to really live here. Imagine that I was free to know you, to love you.'

Love. The word hung in the air, almost physical, he could trace the lines of it.

'I think I've been doing the same thing.'

She looked at him then, and her lip trembled. 'It's a lovely dream. But I'm not Rosy, I can't be. And although I don't and won't ever regret the way you make me feel or the way I feel about you and your girls, my feelings don't change anything.' Her expression was anxious. 'You do understand, don't you?'

Of course he did. He was also a man with commitments and honour and responsibilities, and he knew how that could drive a person. If Rosy had been the kind of woman who put her own needs before those things then she wouldn't be the person he was falling for. It was that integrity he'd first noticed in her, and ironically it was that integrity that meant they could never be.

'How long do we have?'

'A few hours.'

'Right.' He sat for a moment, absorbing this change in events, the feelings coursing through him: disappointment, sadness, the sense that something rare and precious was about to slip through his fingers. But not yet. They still had a few hours. 'Then we'd better not waste them.'

Rosy's troubled expression turned confused, and Jack pushed his chair back, leaving the scone uneaten as he stood and strode over to her, taking her hands in his. 'Jack,' she half whispered, and he captured her mouth with his, urging himself to seize every moment, every sensation, every touch.

'This has been more than just a fling for me,' he said, breaking away to cup her face in his hands.

'Me too. If things were different. But these are the cards we were dealt.'

'We just need to make the best of them.'

She knew him, she understood him, and Jack knew how rare that was. Lily and he had shared passion and built a life together, but she had never understood him and, try as he might, she had eluded his understanding too.

'I wouldn't change a thing either,' she added. 'You're a wonderful father and a wonderful man, Jack. That's why I have come to care for you as much as I do. But…'

'You don't have to say anything else. We both knew that this was a one summer thing. I went into it with my eyes wide open and I wouldn't change a thing.'

'You wouldn't?'

'Well, maybe one thing. If I'd known you were leaving so soon I would have kissed you the first day I met you and not stopped.'

'That might have got awkward. People would have definitely noticed.'

'It would have been worth it.' And then

he did kiss her, slow and sweet, as if they had all the time in the world, not just a few hours, breathing her in, memorising her, trying his best to show her what she meant to him without words. Rosy responded in kind, holding him close so he could feel her imprinted on him. Jack refused to think of the countdown until she had to leave, not deepening the kiss or rushing them, instinctively aware that whatever they did, whatever they said in the hours to come, this right here was the real goodbye.

Rosy filled his senses, her scent, sweet and warm and uniquely her, her taste, the sound of her breath and her occasional murmured endearments, the silk of her skin under his fingers until all he could think of was the here, the now and her.

She pulled back and looked up at him, lips swollen and expression hazy with desire. 'Let's go upstairs,' she said. 'I want you.'

'You have me,' he vowed and swung her into his arms, enjoying her surprised shriek as he carried her upstairs. 'You have me.' And he meant every word. For today at least.

# CHAPTER TEN

'Maman, are you okay?'

As usual Queen Iara was impossible to read. Arrosa's mother had perfected the art of the professional mask a long time ago and Arrosa had never seen it slip. But if she was ever going to falter then today would surely be the day because in less than half an hour the Asturian Royal Family would hold a press conference and announce Clem's existence to the world.

'I'm fine, dear. Clemence is a lovely young woman, and I am happy to be welcoming her into the family.'

'Maman, this is me; you don't have to repeat the press statement.' But they had never had a close relationship, never confided in one another and maybe that was why Arrosa had not told her mother about Jack and how much she missed him.

She'd hoped time would help but although she'd now been apart from Jack for longer than she'd known him, she still felt his absence keenly. She'd been too busy to pine but she couldn't shake the feeling that something was missing, a constant sense of loss. As a result, she'd welcomed her packed diary, preferring to work from the minute she poured her first coffee until she cleaned her teeth at night.

The ratification of the law had gone through unanimously the month before and Arrosa was now the Crown Princess and official heiress to the throne, tripling her workload and responsibilities overnight. She, her father and Clem had discussed making Clem's existence public before the ratification, but Clem had not been ready, nor had she wanted to overshadow Arrosa's big moment. Just knowing that their father was willing to acknowledge her had been enough for her then. But Clem had accepted Arrosa's invitation to stay at the villa and house share with her and, even though the press didn't have access to the estate, Clem's existence was being noticed and questions were being asked, especially as she and Akil were seen more and more in public together.

Once Clem had agreed that she was ready to face the spotlight they had just needed the Queen's agreement for today's announcement. An announcement that would change Clem's life for ever. Arrosa just hoped her sister was ready. And that her mother really was as comfortable with it all as she claimed.

'The past is about to be raked over, that's got to be difficult.'

'Your father's romance was over before we married.' The Queen's smile was serene.

'Barely. And you might not have been formally engaged when he was with Simone, but you had an understanding...'

'Arrosa. Things are different for us, you know this. I didn't love your father when I married him, and I didn't expect him to love me. We married because I knew what being the Queen would entail and I was willing to make the sacrifices necessary. I respected your father and I still do. Clem and her mother didn't change that.'

Was that true? After all, Arrosa's mother hadn't found out about Clem's existence until after she was pregnant with Arrosa and there had been no more children once she was born. Her parents had separate suites of rooms, separate beds. Had they tried for more children or had the realisation that her husband loved another poisoned their marriage, despite her mother's calm words? Once again, she wished she had the kind of relationship with her parents that would enable those questions to be answered.

She laid a hand on her mother's arm, wishing she could give her the kind of easy, warm hug Simone had doled out so easily. 'Well, I just want you to know how much I appreciate it. Thank you for making Clem welcome and agreeing to let her be part of our family in every way. It can't be easy, but it means a lot to me. I hope you know how much.'

'Her mother was very good to you, and I was always grateful for that. You bloomed in Cornwall, would come back refreshed and invigorated—and you did once again this summer. I was pleased to see you looking so well. I had been worried about you but since you returned you seem more like your old self.'

'Thank you.' Arrosa had had no idea that her mother had noticed that she was run-down. Arrosa could feel her cheeks heating as memories of the summer—of Jack—flooded her senses. 'I understand why you always needed your summer retreats now. Time away from the public eye.'

'I accepted a role with certain expectations. I can't complain when those expectations get too much, but a month away every summer ensures I never get overwhelmed by the pressures of my life. And I hope you will always make sure you have time to recharge.

'Things have changed, Arrosa, your new role is testament to that. You don't have to follow the same path your father and I tread; you will be a new kind of monarch in a new Asturia.' Her mother looked over at Clem, who stood in the opposite corner, unusually smart in a blue dress and matching jacket, looking up at Akil with a trust and love that took Arrosa's breath away. 'Your sister's life is about to alter irrevocably but she has you and the Ortiz heir by her side. And after today she can be publicly in your life as you take on your new duties. I know you'll need that support in the years ahead.'

Was that why her mother was agreeing to stand by her husband's side when he announced the existence of a child who wasn't hers, for Arrosa's sake? Arrosa knew her mother loved her, but she was always so hands-off, the thought of her making such a personal sacrifice for her was almost overwhelming. Maybe they could have a warmer, more intimate relationship, maybe it wasn't too late.

'I know the next few weeks will be difficult for us all, especially Clem, but I have to admit I'm happy we won't have to hide any more—and you're right. Having her here in Asturia and openly part of my life will make everything easier.'

'I hope that you will find a different kind of support too, Arrosa. That you will meet a man who looks at you the way Akil Ortiz looks at your sister, who will support you the way he supports her. Being a monarch can be a lonely job but with the right people around you it doesn't have to be that way. Ah, your father is ready. It's time.'

Without a backward glance her mother glided over to Arrosa's father and laid a hand on his arm, her expression calm and inscrutable as ever. Arrosa took a deep breath as she joined her sister, falling in behind her parents and, with a reassuring squeeze of Clem's hand, the four of them made their way out to face the awaiting press.

As expected, the news of Clem's parentage made headline news across the globe. It had,

Akil noted wryly, all the ingredients any good royal scandal needed: a secret love affair, an illegitimate child, a wronged wife standing by her husband's side and two beautiful young women, one a Crown Princess. Any hope that the scandal would be a twenty-four-hour wonder soon disappeared as the world's press descended on Asturia, desperate for a new angle on the story. Descended on Asturia *and* Polhallow, where the cottage was besieged by photographers despite nobody living there, Gus having accompanied Arrosa to Asturia, where he'd promptly taken up residence in her villa.

Arrosa should have foreseen that it was only a matter of time before someone put two and two together and realised that Clem's French cousin Rosy and her royal half-sister were one and the same. Sure enough, a few weeks later, just as the original scandal started to abate, the connection was made, creating a flurry of new headlines and speculation. Sally's family's café was surrounded by reporters wanting the inside scoop on her friendship with both the Princess and Clem, and worse, someone mentioned 'Rosy's' friendship with Jack to one reporter, who immediately splashed the story with suitably salacious headlines.

'Look at this.' Arrosa pushed her tablet over to Clem, her chest tight with anxiety.

'You shouldn't read this stuff, any of it,' Clem said staunchly, but her sister was pale and Arrosa felt a stab of guilt at the world she'd been catapulted into. Adverts Clem had starred in were all over social media, a love scene from a daytime TV show replayed endlessly, her headshots reproduced over and over.

'It's not about me or you. It's Jack.'

'Jack?' Clem's eyebrows shot up. 'Jack Treloar?'

Arrosa had always been able to tell her sister anything, but somehow she'd not found the words to talk about Jack. The memories were too raw, too recent to share, her own feelings so mixed up, especially when Clem and Akil were obviously falling deeper in love every day.

'Yes, we were…friendly.'

'Friendly?' Clem reached over for the tablet. 'How friendly?' She started to read out loud. *'Princess's Summer Fling with Local Bad Boy*—honestly, you babysat for him a couple of times and they turn it into some kind of torrid romance. Listen to this: *'Princess Arrosa enjoyed more than a secret Cornish getaway this summer. We can exclusively reveal that the twenty-six-year-old heir to the Asturian throne enjoyed a summer fling with local self-made millionaire Jack Treloar. Jack, thirty, was married to tragic socialite Lily Fforde-Browne, who overdosed two years ago, leaving two daughters. Now it seems the not-so-grieving widower has moved onwards and upwards. Treloar's teenage marriage to Fforde-Browne raised eyebrows amongst her friends at the time, thanks to his reputation as the town troublemaker, but Treloar put his past behind him, founding Treloar Capital Investments and buying a mansion in London's exclusive Primrose Hill, before moving his family back to Cornwall where they live in a stunning Art Deco house, last valued at a cool three million pounds. The Princess and the rebel are reported to have sneaked away for a romantic getaway on the Isles of Scilly. "They seemed very much in love," said fellow tourist, Lucy Christie. "They couldn't keep their hands off each other."* Honestly, the things they make up!'

Arrosa couldn't answer, her cheeks hot,

and Clem narrowed her eyes. 'Not made up? You and Jack Treloar? It's true? Why didn't you say anything?'

'I don't know,' she said miserably. 'I was going to but there's so much going on it just never seemed relevant.'

'Relevant? You're my sister. What hurts you hurts me. Was it serious?'

'How could it be? You know my life! Jack's so private, he would hate my world.'

'Well, that's unfortunate because right now he's right in the middle of it.'

Clem's words were bracing but her tone sympathetic as Arrosa took the tablet back and read through the article again, cringing at every word. 'So hateful, implying he's some kind of social climber—and mentioning Lily as well. I knew I should have stayed away from him. That there was only one way this could end.'

'In that case why didn't you?'

'I thought that nobody would find out. I thought I deserved the chance to grab some happiness before everything changed. Truth is, Clem, I couldn't help it. Jack's not the man in this article, he's kind and principled and...'

'And drop-dead gorgeous?' her sister helpfully supplied.

Arrosa groaned. 'So gorgeous. I have never in my life wanted anyone the way I wanted Jack. You know, at times I thought there might be something wrong with me. It was so easy to behave like the proper Princess I was expected to be, I was never truly tempted by any man, not enough to let my guard down. And then there was Jack, and it was like *boom*! I couldn't have resisted him if I'd tried—and I didn't try very hard.'

Clem reached over and took her hand. 'You're allowed to be normal, you know. You're allowed to fancy someone, to date, to have romantic getaways.'

'They make it sound so sordid and it wasn't. It was beautiful, Clem.'

'Are you still in touch?'

She shook her head. 'We said we'd try and stay friends but it was too difficult, I couldn't see how to do it. The girls didn't know who I was, although I guess they do now. And the way my life is, it was easier to make a clean break. It was meant to be easier anyway.'

'But you miss him?'

She nodded. 'I really do.'

'You know what I think?'

'I think you're about to tell me.'

'I think I am going to say to you what Akil

said to me and to Zorien.' Clem still didn't call their father *Dad*, maybe she never would. 'Secrets only have power while they're secrets. Once things are out in the open, they can't be used against you. Look, I was thinking we need to help Sally out over the next couple of weeks. She's besieged by reporters; it's impacting on the café and it's scary for Alice. Let's invite her and Jack and all the kids here.'

'Here? To Asturia?'

'Here to the estate. There's plenty of space in the château itself, thanks to all those unused apartments. Your parents are never here, you don't use your rooms and there's the grounds to explore and soldiers on the gates. It's the perfect place to ride out the media interest safely. And with you and Jack in close proximity, well, who knows? At least you'd get a chance to see if there is anything real here.'

Arrosa could see the sense in everything that Clem said, and she should have thought about how to help Sally negotiate the press herself. She did have plenty of room. There were several unused guest apartments in the old medieval Artega palais—and with her villa a mile away, even though it was in the estate grounds, she and Jack wouldn't be forced into proximity. 'But if Jack comes to Asturia everyone will think we're an item and we're not.'

'Well, either we keep it a secret, fly him in quietly and hope no one sees or let them think it. Legitimise the headlines and get rid of the speculation. Seize control of the narrative. Maybe there is more there than a summer fling, maybe not. Either way, you steer the story and get some more time together.'

Arrosa bit her lip. Clem was making sense except… 'He won't come. School's started and the whole thing will be too disorientating for the girls.' Plus, she suspected he was too proud to seek shelter from her. He probably blamed her for setting this circus on him.

'Want to bet?' Clem slid her phone over. It was playing a British news channel showing helicopters circling over Jack's house, photographers at his gate. 'It's October now, nearly half-term, so they wouldn't miss more than a couple of weeks, and I can't imagine they're finding it easy to concentrate with all this going on. Call him and ask him to come. I think he'll say yes.'

'Daddy, Daddy, it's like a fairy tale.' Clover circled a suit of armour a little warily, as if unsure whether it really was inanimate or not. 'This is a real castle!'

Jack had to admit that Clover had a point. It had been late afternoon when the private plane had landed in Asturia and he had glimpsed mountains and valleys, seas and flower-filled villages as the plane had circled before landing. They had been transferred directly into a limousine before being driven through a back gate and straight to the Artega family estate. Soldiers had checked their ID at the imposing gates and then they had been driven for what felt like miles through parkland, woods and formal gardens until they'd reached the old château, graceful with its turrets and spires and carved stonework. It had been a visceral reminder that, although he might now have wealth, he and Arrosa came from worlds apart.

A housekeeper had taken them through the receiving hall and up a grand staircase to an apartment as elegant and well-appointed as any top hotel, where dinner had been served to the by now weary travellers. It hadn't taken Tansy, Clover and Alice long to recover themselves, although he suspected he'd worn an identical shell-shocked expression to Sally throughout the five courses accompanied by some excellent wine, thanks to the juxtaposition of the morning spent escaping the baying photographers and their present situation with candlelight and silver service.

Since Rosy's summer adventures had hit the headlines, it had been an intense couple of days although, to his relief, both girls, even Tansy, seemed to find the whole experience a huge adventure. He'd worried she might feel betrayed by Arrosa's secret but instead she viewed it as impossibly romantic.

It wasn't his first brush with the tabloids and gossip columns, thanks to Lily's bohemian lifestyle and tragic death, but nothing had prepared him for the shock of being in the sightline of the world's media. He could understand Rosy's need for time away now, her determination to keep her stay secret—and her insistence her life wasn't for sharing. Who would willingly put themselves in this position?

'Alice and I are meeting up with Clem this morning to explore. She says she's only walked in a quarter of the grounds at most. Imagine having a place so big you can go for a walk in your own grounds. Apparently, we can swim in the lake as well. Can you believe how warm it is for mid-October?' Sally looked a lot more relaxed this morning. Jack just wished he felt the same way. 'Do you want me to take your girls so you can work— or do you and Rosy have plans?' She sipped her coffee, a demure expression on her face as she waited for his answer.

'She's not Rosy here, she's Arrosa.' Jack poured himself more coffee and surveyed the sumptuous spread of fresh fruit, pastries, cheeses, meats and bread, but despite the tempting smells he had little appetite.

'She's the same person.'

Jack looked around at the silk curtains, the antique furniture, the high ceilings with ornate mouldings, polished wooden floors and vast amounts of gilt. This was a guest apartment—a guest apartment with four bedrooms with en suite bathrooms, a dining room, morning room, formal sitting room and snug. What were the royal apartments like if this was a guest suite? What would it do to a person to be raised amongst all this?

But she didn't live here, she had moved out at twenty-one. And Sally was right. She was still the same person. A person who he was supposedly friends with. A person he had made love to the last time he had seen her.

'If you don't mind having all three?'

'Not at all. Don't feel you have to hurry; Clem and I have a lot of catching-up to do and it will be nicer for Alice if she has friends to play with.'

The girls were delighted with the plan to spend the day exploring, swimming and visiting the stables and getting to meet Clem, who had taken on mythological status in their eyes as she was a real-life actress—Tansy—and a long-lost princess—Clover. Jack let that one stand, he wasn't up to explaining illegitimacy laws and royalty to a six-year-old, leaving him free to follow the path leading to the lake, where Rosy's house was situated. He didn't allow himself to think about how she hadn't been there to meet them, nor how formal she had sounded when she'd called and asked him if he would accompany Sally and Alice to Asturia for a few days until the interest in them died down. Nor did he want to think about how much he'd missed her over the last few months, how often he'd considered picking up the phone, only to remind himself there was no point. Now here he was, in her country, in her grounds, walking to her house.

To his surprise her cottage was charming rather than grand, a one-storey whitewashed villa by the lake, surrounded by a beautiful garden. He took a deep breath and let himself in at the gate and walked down the path. It didn't feel as if he was calling on a princess, there were no visible guards, no servants, but he had no doubt that every step he was taking was being tracked. Before he could knock on the door it opened and there she was.

Jack had no idea why it was a shock that she looked exactly the same—what had he expected, that she would open the door in a ball dress and a crown? It might have been easier if she had because with her hair loose, wearing a green maxi dress cinched in at the waist, she looked like the Rosy he had fallen for, not the Princess he'd said goodbye to three months before.

'Hi,' he said, hovering a few steps away, not wanting to complicate things by touching her, kissing her, not trusting himself not to if he got within touching distance.

'Hi. Do you want some coffee?'

'Sure.'

'Come in then.'

The house was simply but beautifully furnished, wooden furniture polished until it glowed, colourful rugs on the floor, cushions on the grey sofas, pictures on the white walls. Everything was well made and no doubt expensive but also clearly chosen because it was wanted, not because of how much it cost, a landscape next to an abstract, hand-thrown vases next to a stack of books. The scent of coffee permeated the air as she led him through to a light-filled kitchen with French windows that led into the garden, the lake visible beyond.

'Your house is nice,' he said.

'Thank you. I always loved the Cornish house and wanted a similar vibe; I don't have Simone's eye or taste but I'm pretty happy with how it turned out.'

'It's very different to the palace.'

'Oh, dear. I had you put in the Mendoza Suite because it's the least formal, but the décor can be a bit much.'

'The *least* formal?'

'Can't you tell? The gold leaf is pretty pared back.' Her mouth was twitching as he nodded solemnly.

'I thought so.'

And with that the ice was broken and Jack found himself at the table, a coffee in his hands and a plate of pastries before him, his appetite returned, but she was careful to step around him, and he waited for her to take a

pastry before he took his, both equally careful not to touch even by accident.

'I'm so sorry,' Rosy said, taking the seat
opposite him. 'We realised that telling the
world about Clem would send the press sniff-
ing around Polhallow and her life there, but
I hadn't really factored in my unmasking. I
guess I thought I lived so quietly I'd slipped
under the radar. I'm not usually that naïve.
Regardless, I should have prewarned you and
Sally. Planned for this in advance—to be fair,
my father cautioned me that I might be recognised in retrospect and of course he was
right.'

But Jack didn't blame her. 'You *did* warn
me—you made it clear that getting entangled with you came with risks. As for Sally,
her family have been taking full advantage.
They've put tables all over the pavement and
any member of the press trying to get a picture or a quote is forced to buy food. They've
even introduced a Princess Afternoon Tea in
your honour.'

'I'm glad someone's getting some benefit
from this mess. But I am truly sorry, Jack.
The attention must have been scary for the
girls. Are they okay?'

'They are. And thank you for having them

here. It's made the whole thing into a huge adventure.'

'But to be missing school when they were so looking forward to getting settled in.'

'All the headteachers agreed that taking the next couple of weeks off before half-term made sense, it was hard to settle with press at the school gates. They've been set work. It's fine.'

'And you? Are you okay?'

Okay? The whole experience had brought back memories of Lily's death, the most private, difficult moments chronicled in the headlines, but he knew Rosy was feeling guilty enough.

'I'm fine. If it wasn't for the girls, I would have ridden the whole thing out, but it was all a little intense for them.'

'We can make it up to them now they're here. There's loads of fun things for them to do here on the estate and Henri is a master at smuggling people out the gates. I've thought of loads of activities.' Her smile was hopeful.

Jack was sure the girls would want to do every one of them—but the fine line he and Rosy trod was already too blurred. 'I'm sure, but look, you don't have to worry about running after us, you must be far too busy. Just point us in the right direction and we'll be fine. We don't want to encourage more speculation about the two of us after all. Don't get me wrong, I'm grateful for the seamless way your guys extracted us, but the last thing we want to do is encourage any more rumours. No one knows we're here and I'd like to keep it that way. Being seen out with you would be the quickest way to heap fuel onto the fire.'

'Of course. I totally get that. But...' She hesitated, twisting a tendril of hair around her finger.

'But?'

'I can see that you want to just lie low and wait for all this to pass, but there is a good chance that your stay here will leak despite our best efforts.'

That had occurred to him, but he hadn't been able to pass up the chance to give the girls a safe place—or, if he was honest with himself, the chance to see Rosy and make sure she was okay.

'If it makes it easier, we could go somewhere else.'

'Or...' She hesitated again. 'We could give them what they want.'

'What do you mean?'

'Look, the reason everything has gone

so crazy is because the press think they are cracking this huge secret. But if we take control of that secret then there's no reason for them to hound you.'

'Okay,' he said cautiously, trying to figure out exactly what she meant. 'In what way?'

'Well, we could give an interview, say we met through Clem and have been dating for a few months but wanted to keep it quiet until we knew if it was going somewhere. We are seen in public a few times then you go back to the UK and after a few weeks we say it didn't work out and we called it off. It won't stop the press interest completely, I get that, but we control the story. You know, make it all open and out there until they lose interest.'

'Just for show?'

'I guess that's something we could decide. Things ended abruptly between us. We weren't ready. I wasn't ready. I regret that.'

Much as he didn't want to, Jack knew that he had to end the conversation right now before he was tempted into doing something stupid like agreeing to her plan.

'I miss you, Rosy.'

'I miss you too.' Their gazes caught and held, and he drank her in.

'And I understand your reasoning but...'

He saw her straight-backed posture sag just a little as he said *but*. 'I can't do that to the girls. They like you, Rosy. *I* like you, you know that, but I'm a grown man and I can cope with a little heartbreak. They can't.'

But how he wanted to agree. How he wanted to spend time with her as if it were still the summer, be with her openly, hold her hand and kiss her and make love to her. Because after all it was the fish and chip loving, ice cream eating, denim shorts and bikini-clad Rosy he'd fallen for. Surely spending time with the Princess in her formal world would be the cure he needed? But it was too much of a risk—and not just for his girls.

'I appreciate you giving us a place to lie low for a while and I know the girls can't wait to see you, but let's think of another way to put a stop to the rumours.'

'Of course.' Her smile was determinedly bright. 'It was just an idea. What are you thinking?'

'Well, the theatre, for example.' Inspiration hit him. 'After all, we're all connected to it. Who's to say that's not why you were in Pol-hallow this summer? Nobody has any proof that we *were* together, apart from a woman who thinks she saw us and a few rumours.

Let the romance talk die a death but use it to do something good for Polhallow instead.'

She stared at him for a long moment, her expression unreadable before nodding. 'Yes, that makes sense.'

'Good, well, let me make some plans. Thank you for the coffee. I'd better get back.'

'Sure.'

He sat there for a moment, wishing for one moment things were different. Jack knew that he was about to turn his back on an opportunity that would never present itself again, turn down the second chance that he had been dreaming of in his heart of hearts.

'Okay. I'll see you soon. No, don't get up, I'll see myself out. Thanks for the coffee.'

As Jack shut the front door behind him he couldn't shake the image of Rosy, straight-backed again, a serene expression on her face, only a hint of a shadow in her eyes giving any hint that she wasn't completely happy with his decision. He could tell himself with perfect truth that all his reasons for saying no were to do with the girls. After all, the last couple of days had been bewildering, terrifying and out of control. They'd had to flee their home, seek sanctuary in a strange country. If this was just what the rumour of a romance between himself and a princess could do, what would any confirmation of that rumour provoke? No, better to let all the speculation die down and return to their normal life as soon as possible.

But Jack was also aware enough to know that there was more to his decision. He'd been burned before, and he couldn't risk being burned again. Of course, he absolved Rosy from having similar motives to Lily. She wasn't looking to shock anyone, to rebel against her parents and societal position, but if they were together, for whatever reasons, it would still be a mésalliance. Nobody in her world would think him a suitable consort for their Crown Princess. He had no idea about court life, he knew nothing about Asturia—until a couple of months ago he couldn't have pointed it out on the map—he didn't speak the language, didn't know the customs. If he was with Rosy, in reality or pretence, then he would be repeating the same pattern as before, be completely out of place, a scandalous object of interest.

None of Lily's friends had believed that she was seriously considering marrying him. Boys like Jack, he'd heard one of her friends say, were perfectly acceptable for messing around with—after all, everyone knew that boys with everything to prove were the best lovers—but one simply didn't marry them. He'd done everything in his power to prove every single one of them wrong and he still got a visceral sense of satisfaction when *they* now courted him, asked him to dinner parties, solicited his advice and sought his investments. But he'd never forgotten how they'd made him feel. Vowed never to be put in that situation again.

And that was why he had to walk away. Because here she wasn't Rosy, she was the Crown Princess, and girls like her simply weren't for guys like him.

# CHAPTER ELEVEN

'DID YOU SEE JACK?' Clem asked when she returned to the villa that evening. Sharing a home with her sister was something Arrosa wasn't sure she would ever take for granted. She would never not appreciate having Clem on hand to laugh with, cry with, watch meaningless television with, chat through her problems with.

It wasn't just the companionship; she was so proud of her sister it almost hurt. Clem had risen above the headlines and started to carve out her own identity here in Asturia. She was looking at university courses, still volunteering at the local hospital and was officially assisting Arrosa. She was also dipping her toes into court life and had been invited to a ball at the British Embassy in a week's time.

But, of course, the downside to having her sister so close was that she knew Arrosa better than anyone and there was no dissembling, no hiding behind her princess face.

'He turned me down.' Some of the heartbreak she didn't want to admit even to herself cracked through the armour she had donned and quickly she added, 'It's complicated. It's fine. I expected it. It's probably for the best.'

'Okay.' Clem poured them both a glass of wine and nodded towards the garden. 'It's still so warm out even if it is October. Shall we?'

With unspoken accord the sisters headed down to the lake. They shared a deep love of water, and both felt better when they were gazing into it. They sat on the comfortable chairs Arrosa kept on the jetty and Clem sniffed the wine before taking an appreciative sip.

'This is much needed; three children are a lot for a full day! But it's so nice to see Sally. I've asked her to come to the ball with me. Akil is attending, but in a work capacity, and I could do with moral support—and she could do with an evening off.'

'Sounds good. And what did you think of Tansy and Clover?' Arrosa half held her breath as she waited for her sister's reply. It really mattered that Clem liked them, she realised.

'They're nice girls, a credit to their dad. And they're both wild about you. I was a pretty poor substitute. They kept asking when they would see you.'

Arrosa stared down at her wine. 'I'm not sure that's such a good idea. Jack made it clear there's no future for us. I don't want to complicate things further.'

'I met him too, back at the château.'

Arrosa couldn't bring herself to ask what Clem thought of Jack. 'He's right, you know. If we tried to control this thing by saying we were in a relationship, by trying out being in a relationship, it would just confuse the girls, and that's the last thing they need. He wants them to have stability and I support that, I always have.'

'He's obviously a great dad. I have to admit it, I got him wrong. He's not the overbearing tycoon I expected but, from what you and Sally say and the little I've seen, he seems a surprisingly kind man. A principled man who I would guess is also clearly head over heels about you and I know you feel the same way. So what I don't understand is why you are both so sure that you have no future.'

'He doesn't want the kind of life I lead, Clem, not for him, not for his girls, and I don't blame him.'

Clem sipped her wine and sat back, her expression thoughtful. 'Rosy, is your life really so bad? I know it got a little overwhelming recently, but I would say that Asturia allows its high-profile people more privacy than many other countries, and the world's press will get bored with this story eventually. I'm not saying that if you gave it another go the first few weeks and months wouldn't be a challenge, but after that I think you could build a pretty decent life here. I should know! It's easier for me in some ways, my education included handling publicity, I know how to work the camera, speak in palatable soundbites and ensure my social media is squeaky clean and, yes, I admit I've still been overwhelmed. But there's been beauty amongst the madness and I'm seeing my way to a future, the opportunities my position gives me. That could be true for Jack as well.'

How Rosy wished her sister was right.

'But you wanted to be part of the family, Jack doesn't. He has some past experiences which make him shy away from publicity, from high profile relationships. He thinks we're better denying everything, using his investment in the theatre as a pretext for our friendship. I owe him that, Clem.'

'The theatre?'

'I haven't really had a chance to discuss it with you, but I think you will love what he has in mind, that Simone would have too. If we say that we were working together on the theatre in memory of your mother, that gives me a reason to have spent the summer in Cornwall and to have been seen with Jack. And in the end Polhallow will have the kind of theatre Simone would have been proud of. It all makes sense.'

But Arrosa knew she was trying to convince herself as well as her sister, was trying not to think about how differently she could have played the morning's conversation. Because absence really had made her heart grow fonder. The moment Jack had walked through the door her home had felt complete.

She'd known what he was thinking, could have sworn that her heart beat in time with his, and she knew that if she'd just reached out, had just touched him, that everything would be different and he would be hers, for now at least.

But she wanted him to come to her because

that was where he wanted to be, not seduced into intimacy. The theatre was a worthy project. It gave them an angle. It was a memorial, and these were all good things. Just because her whole being ached with sadness and loss didn't change any of those things.

'Look,' Clem said, putting her glass down. 'Whatever you decide I will support, I hope you know that. But if having Jack in your life is what you want, and if having Jack by your side makes your difficult role an iota easier, then you should fight for that, Rosy. You have always done what's right, you always put other people first. Maybe now is the time to concentrate on you. I believe you deserve someone by your side who sees how special you are. If that person is Jack then don't let him walk away because he doesn't understand your life. Show him how he fits in. Show him that your life has magic as well as duty. I get how he feels. I didn't want to stay here as Akil's mysterious English lover. I had to figure out how I could be here as me and I found that. But I didn't find it alone—Akil helped me. You don't have to do this alone either, nor does Jack. Just promise me you'll think about it.'

Arrosa blinked, her eyes hot and heavy

with tears she refused to shed. Was it simply as easy as deciding she wanted Jack in her life? How could it be?

'I'll think about it. Thank you, Clem.'

Her sister smiled affectionately. 'What are sisters for?'

Over the next ten days Arrosa did more than think. Instead of hiding away from Jack and the girls she made time in her hectic schedule to show Jack exactly what made her country so special and why she loved it so much. The girls were usually busy during her pockets of free time, once, to her amazement, with her parents, who had never been the kind to spend time with children before. She suspected Clem of making sure Jack was on his own when she was able to join him, but her sister denied the charge with an innocent look that didn't fool Arrosa one jot. But she wasn't complaining because, whatever the reason behind Tansy and Clover's busy schedule, it left her free to smuggle Jack out with her bodyguard, Henri's, help to show him the country she loved and the work that was needed to bring it properly into the twenty-first century. Just as she'd hoped, Jack was soon filled with enthusiasm and ideas for how things could be improved.

They weren't long excursions, just a few hours here and there, never a full day, although there was some time in every day, but in those moments she was the perfect blend of Arrosa and Rosy, princess and person, and she could feel herself falling harder and harder for Jack. But although he seemed to enjoy their time together, there was still a chasm between them. They didn't touch, and never alluded to any kind of future together. It was as much torture as it was joy. It was all she had.

She walked into the house late one afternoon, looking for Clem, who was getting ready for the ball at the British Embassy. She found her sister in her room, putting the last touches to her hair and make-up, a stunning red floor-length cocktail dress hanging ready.

Arrosa whistled in appreciation. 'You look amazing.'

'Thank you. It feels odd to be there as an Asturian representative.'

'You'll be brilliant.'

Clem sucked in a breath. 'I'm glad I persuaded Sally to come, she deserves some fun and I could do with the backup. How was your day?'

'Good. I spent the morning going over

my speech for the day after tomorrow and in meetings then I took Jack on my favourite mountain walk. I needed the exercise. You know, even though it's still quite warm, I can feel winter in the air. Those trails will be under snow within a month.'

It had been a lovely walk but sometimes Arrosa wondered what she and Jack were doing. They seemed no further forward. If anything, they seemed to be slipping away from each other every time they spent a polite, distanced time together.

Clem swivelled round on her stool. 'It's been over a week, Rosy. Have you told Jack how you feel yet?'

'I…'

'Told him that you love him?' her sister went on remorselessly.

Arrosa stared at her and swallowed. 'Love? I…' But she'd stopped lying to herself a long time ago, she wouldn't lie to her sister. 'I've told him that I like him, Clem, he knows how much I fancy him…' *Fancy.* Such a trite word to describe the depth of longing she felt whenever he was near. 'I think we both know that it might have been love if things were different but, after all, we've not really known each other that long.'

'About as long as I've known Akil,' her sister reminded her.

There was no point quibbling or reminding Clem that she and Akil had spent far more time together because she knew it had taken just a few weeks for her sister and friend to fall firmly and irrevocably in love. To forge the kind of partnership Arrosa had only ever dreamed of.

'I can't.'

'Rosy. This last week and a half you've been lit up with happiness and I know it's not because you're finally addressing the Senate in two days' time! It's thanks to Jack, and he deserves to know the truth.'

'I've seen him every day and he's made no attempt to even touch me. He likes Asturia and he has ideas, good ones, but he hasn't offered any more than those thoughts. It's obvious he doesn't see a future here. And, even if he did, there's the girls. Who knows, maybe we can try again when they are grown up, maybe in ten years or so.' The thought was bleak indeed and her chest constricted at the thought of spending those years alone.

'In a decade? Come on, Rosy, listen to yourself.'

'Clem, you don't understand. If I told him

how I feel then I am forcing him to make a choice. His marriage was hard, Lily manipulative at best, I think. It wasn't a happy marriage, Clem. She used him. I won't do that to him.'

Clem sighed. 'Rosy, have you ever thought that by not being honest with him maybe you're the one doing the manipulating? That maybe you're the one depriving him of agency. He should know how you feel. Tell him.'

Jack had enjoyed the last twelve days almost too much, and the more time he spent with Rosy, seeing Asturia through her eyes, the more he could see her hopes and dreams. More, in every project and plan he saw ways he could contribute, how he could be an integral part of her world. But still he hesitated. This was no more real life than Cornwall had been, their friendship still kept firmly under wraps.

If friendship was what this was. The air between them was still charged although there was no intimacy, but he was still more relaxed with Rosy than with anyone else, than he had ever been with another person.

There were still some intrepid photogra-

phers hanging around the Palais walls, trying
to photograph every car that left the house,
but Henri was an old hand at shaking off unwanted attention and some days Jack and the
girls were completely free to wander around
and explore with nobody giving them more
than a quick half amused sideways look.

And the more he explored, the more he fell
in love with the small country. He loved the
crispness of the mountain air as early autumn
which felt more like an English late summer
softened and cooled. The actual autumn was
short, with snow usually expected by Decem-
ber. This, of course, sent the girls into spirals
of excitement and they begged to be able to
stay until the snow came. Every day he had
to remind himself as much as them that this
was just a visit, that they were establishing
their lives in Polhallow. Somehow his plans
didn't feel certain as they had before, that
sense of rightness that had driven the move
eluding him.

And, of course, there was Rosy. His tour
guide, filled with infectious excitement about
her country and the plans she had to improve
it. She seemed to know every hidden corner
and selflessly shared them with him.

They had successfully renegotiated their

relationship from lovers into friends, and that, he knew, was rare and precious. But he still felt an almost overwhelming sense of loss when he stood next to her but couldn't hold her, when he said goodbye but didn't kiss her, alone in his huge luxury bed.

'Look, Daddy!' Clover pointed at the TV. 'There's Rosy.'

He'd found a cable channel of English language children's programmes and Clover and Alice had been curled up in front of a film while he packed for an afternoon on the beach, but somehow the channel had switched to a local news one. The anchor was speaking about this historic day in the fast-paced Spanish-accented French dialect he was slowly starting to understand. This was the day Arrosa was finally presented to Parliament as the Crown Princess and heir to the throne.

Jack had learnt a lot about Asturian customs and politics over the last few days and knew that, unlike the UK, the Asturian monarch sat in the Senate, their Upper Chamber, and was very much engaged in Parliamentary procedure. When he chose, the King could deputise his heir to step in for him—and now she was officially the heir that meant Rosy, who today was taking her place as the Royal representative. Custom dictated that a new member of the Senate would need to be presented, approved and welcomed by the House before giving their first speech.

Jack knew how nervous Rosy felt. She was no stranger to politics or public speaking, but this was her first formal step into her country's political arena. It was a relief to see Akil, a prominent member of the opposition and a fellow member of the Senate, was there, looking strong and supportive, and to hear the whole chamber burst into applause as she entered.

Jack stared at the screen, his heart hammering, mouth dry. This was not Rosy, this was all Arrosa. Her hair was up in a complicated knot and she wore a calf-length blue silk dress with a short matching jacket, diamonds at her throat and in her ears, a crown perched on the top of her head. She could almost have come straight out of the fairy tales Clover adored.

'She looks beautiful,' Clover said breathlessly.

'Yes, but she looks scared too,' Tansy said.

'No, she doesn't,' Alice chimed in and Sally laid a hand on her daughter's head.

'Why do you think that, Tansy?'

Tansy studied the screen. 'Her hands are pressed together, and she bit her bottom lip just then. She does that when she's nervous, have you noticed?'

Jack *had* noticed, but he was surprised his daughter had. 'You're right,' he said. 'But she hides it well. That's very astute of you, Tansy.'

His oldest daughter tossed her hair. 'I'm an actress,' she told him. 'Studying people is what I do.'

He laughed but quickly quietened as Rosy started to speak. There was no trace of any nervousness in her voice as she spoke, her voice rich and melodious. Her father beamed proudly from behind her.

The family had plans for the day. With their time in Asturia nearing its end there was plenty they still wanted to pack in, but Jack forgot to hurry the girls up or to gather his own things together. Instead, he stood transfixed as he watched the woman he loved address the country she was born to rule.

The chasm between them had never felt bigger and yet in some ways he felt that he should and could almost step into the TV to stand beside her and support her just with his presence. Jack had been telling himself over the last twelve days that Rosy needed a man like Akil. She needed someone versed in Asturia's culture and politics, someone with a background similar to hers. But as he stood watching her speak that certainty escaped him.

Culture and nationality and birthright were all important and all things he lacked, but he did have qualities he knew she needed. He could provide her with the reassurance that she could do the immense job that lay ahead of her, he could be the person she bounced ideas off—after all, she had run every word of her speech past him, practised it on him until he could probably recite it himself in Asturian and English, could have cited her sources as she focused on education, equality and the need for a sustainable future.

But, at the same time, although they had spent a great deal of time together there was a consciousness between them that hadn't been there before. Rosy was her usual thoughtful, enthusiastic self, unfailingly courteous, great with the girls as always, funny and sweet, but he knew he wasn't imagining the distance between them, and he wasn't sure who was responsible for it. In some ways he welcomed it. After all, there was no future for them.

But the knowledge didn't feel as certain as it once had. The future he'd mapped out no longer felt so safe or so desirable. Instead it felt empty. Lonely. His girls were everything, but they would grow up and have their own lives and that was how it should be. And when they were gone what would he have? A white box on the top of a cliff, a self-made fortune and no one to share either with.

Rosy's speech was coming to an end. Her pace had quickened, her tone reaching an emotional peak before calming once again as she laid down her notes and gazed confidently into the camera, just the pink in her cheeks betraying her nervousness. There was no need as the chamber erupted into applause and a few whoops. She bowed her head respectfully to the chamber of men—and it was still all men—before retaking her seat. Jack could see her father—King Zorien—in the background, also clapping along, his face red with pride, but as he struggled to his feet the colour seemed to drain from his face and, to Jack's horror, he sank back down again, hands pressed to his chest.

Time seemed to stop as the applause stilled

and all eyes focused on the clearly struggling King, the camera cutting away as Arrosa sank to her knees beside her father, fear evident on her face.

And Jack knew one thing. None of the barriers or problems or reasons to keep his distance mattered. Rosy needed him; it was as simple as that.

# CHAPTER TWELVE

ARROSA HAD NEVER spent much time in hospitals before, apart from as a royal visitor, there to cut ribbons and talk to pre-selected patients, and she was more grateful than ever for the presence of Clem and Akil. Thanks to their volunteer work, they were both well-known and familiar with the city hospital and on friendly terms with many of the staff.

Her father had been rushed to the private rooms reserved for the Royal Family and other VIP patients but, even with the comforting décor and peace, it was clear that this was a medical facility not a five-star hotel. The lingering smell was one of boiled vegetables and antiseptic, there were medical instruments evident all around and she knew that, even though she was in a plushly furnished sitting room, the tight ball of dread preventing her breathing properly was the same as that in the chests of everyone waiting in the wards and family rooms across the wider hospital.

Her father had been rushed straight into emergency surgery. Arrosa had tried to take in the words from the family liaison nurse, words like *heart* and *bypass* and *serious*, but she couldn't concentrate. Her mother had been at a prearranged event at the other side of the country. Although Arrosa knew she was sorry to have missed her speech, she hadn't wanted to let the school down, duty as important to Queen Iara as family. She had been informed about the incident straight away and was on her way back, so all Arrosa could do was pace and sit, pace and sit and let the various hot drinks cool untouched.

'Go home and rest,' Clem said, taking her hand. 'Or at least change.' Arrosa touched her hair, almost surprised to feel the cold of the platinum crown on her head. The morning's speech felt like a lifetime ago. She removed it with shaky hands, her head instantly lighter, and pulled out the hairpins keeping her hair confined in the intricate knot, pulling it back into a loose ponytail instead.

'I can't leave him.'

'Then at least try and drink something.'

And to please her sister Arrosa managed

a couple of sips of coffee before her stomach tightened and she couldn't swallow any more.

She paced over to the window and stared out at the hospital grounds, the trees now turning to orange, red and yellow, seeing her sister and Akil reflected in the glass. They were sitting together on the sofa, Clem leaning into Akil, his comforting arms around her shoulders. For one brief, shameful moment she felt a pang of such pure envy it shocked her out of her stupor. Not for Clem's happiness, that was something that filled her with joy, but because she wanted something similar for herself. Because she'd been so close to having something similar, but life and obligation and cowardice had pushed it away.

At that moment the door opened and she whirled around, expecting to see a doctor. Instead, Henri walked in, followed by the one person she realised she needed more than anyone else.

'Jack?' Had she dreamed him? But no, he felt solid enough as she ran to him, and he pulled her against him. 'You came.'

'I didn't want to intrude,' he said, looking uncharacteristically diffident, and she reached up to touch his cheek.

'You're not intruding, you never could.'

He led her to the sofa opposite Clem and Akil and pulled her down to sit next to him. 'How's your father?'

'It's not good, Jack. They rushed him straight in for bypass surgery. It's his heart.'

'I see.'

'His *heart*, Jack. It's like history repeating itself. You know his father abdicated because of *his* heart and then he died anyway, just a couple of years later. What if…?' She broke off, swallowing back almost hysterical tears. 'I can't lose him yet. I'm not ready.'

Then Jack's arms were around her, pulling her in tight, holding her, allowing her the freedom to let go, to be supported. She was dimly aware of Clem and Akil muttering something about going to get coffee and food and then she and Jack were alone and for the first time in a long time she allowed herself the luxury of tears. Once she'd started, she couldn't stop, all her fears and worries and regrets mingling with the shock and worry for her father's health and what that meant for the whole family, for her.

Arrosa had no idea how long she cried. When she finally choked back a last sob she was cradled in Jack's arms, his shirt wet through, a damp tissue clasped in her hands.

'I'm sorry. Look at your shirt,' she said, pulling back a little.

'I'm used to it,' he said, and his smile was tender. 'I have a six-year-old.'

'I didn't mean…'

He shook his head. 'Never apologise to me for having emotions, Rosy. You're allowed to be scared and upset and all that entails.'

'My father has dedicated his whole life to duty. He needs more time to live, not just be. He and Clem have only just started building a relationship. It would break her heart if anything happened to him before she really got to spend time with him.'

'And what about you?'

'Me?'

'Like I said, you're allowed to have feelings too, especially around me.'

Arrosa buried her head in his shoulder, her voice muffled when she did speak. 'I feel so selfish to be thinking of me at a time like this.'

'But?'

'Oh, Jack. My father was around my age when he had to become King, and because of that he left Clem's mother, left Clem, and married Maman, and they haven't had a happy marriage. Instead he dedicated his life to service, as did she. I know that is my future, I've come to terms with it, but I'm not ready, not yet. And…' She almost choked back the next words but she made herself keep going. 'I don't want to do it alone. I know I have Clem, but…' She couldn't quite bring herself to say the words quivering on her tongue. To say that she didn't want to do this without Jack. To tell him that having him here by her side, in her country was more than she had ever wished for, hoped for.

To tell him that she loved him.

But this wasn't the time and place.

'I'm sorry. I'm being cowardly and weak.'

Jack took her hands in his. 'Arrosa Artega, you're the bravest person I know.'

But she wasn't being brave now, was she? 'I…'

Before she could say anything else Clem and Akil arrived back with fresh hot drinks and an array of food. To her surprise, Arrosa discovered that she was a little hungry and managed half a roll and some of the coffee but the time to confide in Jack had passed. The day stretched on as the minutes slowly ticked by and there was still no news of her father.

Her mother arrived soon after Clem returned and Arrosa was both surprised and moved by the Queen's evident distress. In some ways it seemed that the events of the last few weeks had brought the royal couple closer together, which made it even more imperative that her father should make a swift and full recovery. If she had to take on more responsibility to enable that to happen then of course she would. She wanted her parents to have the time to enjoy this new understanding between them, for her father and Clem to have the time to develop a proper relationship, for her father to be able to enjoy his grandchildren when they finally came along. She was prepared to do whatever she needed to do to enable that. But she knew now that it would be easier with Jack by her side.

Clem was right. Arrosa had thought she was protecting Jack by hiding her feelings from him but, really, she was disempowering him. He deserved the chance to know how she felt and to make his own decisions.

It felt like an age before the doctor came in, removing his mask and rubbing his eyes wearily. 'I'm pleased to say that the operation went as well as could be expected,' he said. 'We're not out of the woods yet, but I'm as cautiously optimistic as I can be. His Majesty is sleeping now and although I can allow

Her Majesty a few minutes at his side if she wishes, I suggest the rest of you go home, get some sleep and return to see him tomorrow.'

The Queen waved off their suggestion that they waited for her, insisting that her car and driver were waiting and she would rather be alone tonight anyway. Arrosa lingered, knowing her mother's tendency to hide behind what she thought she should do rather than what she wanted, but her mother met her gaze firmly and nodded.

'You too, Arrosa,' she said. 'You've had an exceptionally busy day. Go and get some rest.'

Her hug was warmer and more heartfelt than usual and Arrosa impulsively pressed a quick kiss to her mother's smooth cheek before allowing Henri to escort her out of the room, Jack closely behind.

Jack stayed in the car until they drew up outside Arrosa's villa, rather than asking to be dropped off at the palace. He checked in with Sally from the car, relieved when she reassured him that the girls were fine and although they were naturally worried about Arrosa and the King, who they had all met and liked, she had managed to distract them for most of the day. They were currently en-

joying dinner in front of the television after
an afternoon at the beach and barely mus-
tered up the energy to shout hellos when she
prompted them. Sally finished by telling him
not to hurry back, and that she was happy to
look after Tansy and Clover for as long as he
needed her to. Jack said a few words of heartfelt gratitude before, with a nod at Henri, following Arrosa into her home. He took her bag
out of her unprotesting fingers and set it on
the hallway table.

'Go on,' he said. 'Go and get changed. That
dress is beautiful, and you look beautiful, but
it doesn't look that comfortable.'

She laughed a little shakily. 'You know, I
spent the first hour we were at the hospital
still wearing a crown. Isn't that ridiculous?'

'For anybody else, maybe.'

'Par for the course for me?' She made no
move away, but stood looking up at him, confusion and hope in her eyes. 'He is going to
be all right, isn't he, Jack?'

'The doctor seemed optimistic. That's en-
couraging.'

'Yes. Thank you for coming, Jack.'

'Any time.'

'Do you want a drink?' She was nervous,
he realised as she whirled into the kitchen and

found him a beer, grabbing one for herself, opening the back doors and ushering him outside. The evenings were chilly now but she didn't seem to feel the cold as she stood staring out at the lake.

'Jack,' she said at last, turning to him. 'When you arrived at the hospital I realised you were exactly who I needed. That you are always who I need. I can't let you go without telling you how I feel. I love you, Jack, with all my heart. I tried not to, but I can't help it.'

Jack stood there, unable to move or speak as each word sank in, warming him through, bringing him to life like soft rain on parched earth.

'I know what the papers say, and how you feel, that my world isn't yours, but I don't believe that. To me you are the knight in shining armour I didn't believe existed. A man who is kind and dependable and who understands me. A man I can trust with every thought and emotion. A man who has proved that over and over. I know you come as part of a package, and I love that too—but I also know that's why you are wary. If this life isn't for you then I will never blame you for that, but I had to tell you how I feel. I want you in my life for ever, you and the girls. I love you.'

'Oh, Rosy. I love you too. I think I have done from the moment you bought us ice cream and saved me from a full-on meltdown.' Jack inhaled, long and deep, searching for the right words. 'I wasn't going to say anything today. I thought what with the speech as well as your father you'd probably had all the emotion you could handle but, as usual, I underestimated you.'

She laughed and took a step closer. Deliberately, Jack took her undrunk beer from her hand and set it down on the garden table next to his and entwined his fingers through hers. The simple act of holding hands after so many weeks apart was like a balm to his soul.

'I told myself I had to stay away for the girls' sake,' he told her honestly. 'And there was truth in that, but I was also hiding behind them. My experience of marrying someone from a different world to me was difficult. My marriage brought me my girls but little happiness. I had to prove myself every day, and still I knew that to the world I was an interloper. I knew if I was with you it would be a thousand times worse. A boy from my background daring to court the Crown Princess? I don't care what the papers say about me, what the Court says, but I care about you.

I didn't want you put in a difficult position. I didn't want you to ever regret choosing me.'

There it was, Jack's truth, and Arrosa knew how privileged she was to hear it.

'I will never regret choosing you,' she told him, cupping his cheek and luxuriating in the rough stubble under her fingers, losing herself in the heat in his eyes. 'Never. The Court will say how clever I am to have snared a man who has made a fortune in such a short time and will wonder how we can best use your talents here, and the papers will come around, they always do. But even if they didn't, I wouldn't care. I know the truth and that's all that matters. But the girls, Jack, if we do this then you would have to be here. Would that work, would they mind?' With the headiness of the relief over her father and the knowledge that Jack loved her, the practicalities of their situation had been too easy to ignore.

'The girls love you and they love it here. There's an international school in the city with a great reputation and they have been begging to stay until the snow comes. It won't always be easy. Tansy is so nearly a teenager, there are bound to be storms ahead…'

'But if we navigate them together…'

'Then nothing is impossible.' He smiled

down at her and she found herself laughing in giddy relief.

'Does that mean you'll stay?'

'It means that I will be looking for a place for me and the girls in the city...'

'But...' she interjected, and he put a finger on her lips.

'Get them settled in school and start to figure out my life here. And while I'm doing that, I want to do some old-fashioned courting. I know I could stay in the apartment where we are, and I am getting rather fond of all those ancestors of yours even if every male is brandishing a sword in a threatening manner and every woman a fan in an even scarier manner, and I am sure you would welcome us here, but Rosy, I rushed into one marriage. This time I want to take my time.'

'You do?' She completely understood—and courting did sound like fun. 'What do you have in mind?'

'The usual. Dinner, walks, theatre trips.' His voice deepened. 'Kissing, I think there should be lots of kissing.'

'Me too.'

'And touching.' Her knees weakened at the intent in his smile. 'Lots and lots of touching.'

'I could get on board with that.' They were

so close now there was no space between them, her arms wound around his neck, her body pressed to his. 'What else?'

'I think I will have to show you.'

She laughed out loud as he swung her up into his arms, carrying her towards the kitchen. 'You might have to show me every day.'

'Oh, I intend to.' And then his mouth was finally on hers and Arrosa could lose herself in his kiss, his scent, the surety of his touch. With Jack by her side, she could face anything, any future, any obstacle. It was more than she had ever dared to dream of, and she couldn't have been more excited about what the future held.

# EPILOGUE

'THE THEATRE looks stunning, Jack.'

Arrosa squeezed Clem's hand gratefully. Even though her sister had become close to Jack and the girls over the last year she knew Clem still struggled with the changes to her mother's restoration work, even with the lack of facilities and comfort in the original theatre. But Jack had worked miracles and the theatre had come alive in the way he had envisioned, from comfortable backstage areas to tempt the biggest stars to Cornwall, to a café open all year round, a fancy restaurant with sea views and a beautiful bar area. The seats were still the original carved stone and open to the air, but patrons could rent or buy seat pads and the theatre sold long raincoats for the times the elements didn't cooperate.

They were here for the official opening night, a Gala in Simone's honour for the local hospice, for which they had all combined their resources to lure in some big names to perform songs, musical theatre numbers, dances and scenes from Shakespeare.

The eight of them sat in the newly created Royal Box, with an actual roof and cushioned seat, its own dining room and cloakroom. Jack had created several of these VIP areas with an eye on the hospitality market and Arrosa was grateful for the shelter even as she looked nostalgically across at the seat where she had met Jack for the first time.

'Do you wish you were performing, Clem?' Queen Iara asked. Arrosa still couldn't believe her mother had asked to attend the Gala in honour of her husband's great love, but she had insisted she wanted to get to know the town where her daughter had been so happy—and to pay homage to the woman who had loved her daughter so selflessly. She and Zorien had the seats of honour at the front and Arrosa was sure she had seen them hold hands earlier—and not for the first time.

'Part of me does,' Clem admitted, her hand straying to her stomach. Akil had not been able to keep his word to wait a year before he proposed, and the pair had married in the spring with their first child expected at Christmas. Arrosa couldn't wait to be an aunt—a hands-on acknowledged aunt who would always be part of the baby's life. 'But it is fun to be in the audience too. I'm just glad the community group still gets to use this space. Thank you, Jack.'

'The theatre wouldn't exist without the community—and I wouldn't have met Rosy either. I'm just glad we had a happier outcome than Romeo and Juliet.' Jack reached for her hand and smiled and Arrosa leaned over to kiss his cheek.

'Me too.' She looked down at her engagement ring, loving the way the rubies caught the light. Jack had stayed in Asturia and they had spent the past nine months really getting to know one another over a slow, sweet courtship which had given the girls plenty of time to adjust to their new lives in Asturia. Jack had proposed a couple of weeks ago, a year to the date they had met, with Clover and Tansy's help in a play the three had written and performed for her. Arrosa couldn't have imagined a more perfect proposal—or a more perfect ring, picked out by the girls for her.

The girls sat next to the King and Queen, bickering amicably over the programme. Over the last year Tansy had lost the last of her worried look and now had a social life to rival Arrosa's and was pursuing acting in the youth theatre in Asturia, while Clover had developed a love of horse riding, never happier than when they were at the Artega estate and she could spend the day in the stables. Both girls would be bridesmaids at the wedding in early autumn, with Clem as maid of honour.

'A toast.' Akil handed around the glasses of champagne, with elderflower cordial for the girls and Clem. 'To Simone, who I wish I had been able to meet, and her legacy.'

'To Simone,' they all chorused, even Queen Iara, while Clem held her cordial up to the sky, where the first stars were visible.

'To Mum.'

'And to Cornwall,' Arrosa added. Clem had decided to keep the cottage so her baby would get to know the village she loved so much. Jack had sold his dream home, reassuring her that his dreams had changed, but the pair could borrow the cottage whenever they wanted, with Henri always on hand to ensure their privacy was respected.

'And to the Asturians for making us so welcome,' Jack finished. 'Thank you for letting us be part of your family.'

'Thank you for letting me be part of yours,'

Arrosa replied and as he leaned over to kiss her she made a mental note to never forget this feeling, surrounded by those she loved and who loved her, in a place dedicated to a woman who had helped raise her. Just a year ago Arrosa had felt completely alone, with the weight of the country on her shoulders. Now look at her, engaged, a stepmother, a soon-to-be aunt.

As the stage lights blazed to life and the show began, she sent a small prayer of thanks to the heavens. Nothing was impossible as long as she was with those she loved, and right now Arrosa Artega, Crown Princess of Asturia, knew she was the luckiest woman alive.

\* \* \* \* \*

*If you enjoyed this story, check out these other great reads from Jessica Gilmore*

Cinderella and the Vicomte
Christmas with His Cinderella
Winning Back His Runaway Bride
Mediterranean Fling to Wedding Ring

*All available now!*